PRAISE FOR

Enchanted Everglades: Friend for Life

★ "With its **imaginative** tapestry of **adventurous** humans, anthropomorphized creatures, and **well-paced action**, Enchanted Everglades **will please middle-grade readers**. But its **poignant lessons** could also draw teachers or mentors interested in sharing the importance of finding peace within both nature and ourselves."

~ BlueInk Review, starred review

❀

"Tween readers (and their parents and teachers) will **love** the values, hardships, laughs, and learning in Kowatch's **thoughtful adventure fantasy**."

~ Booklife Reviews

❀

"Readers who enjoy a **blend of realism and fantasy** are sure to be drawn to this **adventurous story** of loss, forgiveness, and mindfulness."

~ The Children's Book Review

❀

"The rich descriptions of wildlife ecosystems make this book **worth reading by all audiences** . . . the action does have a cartoonish, made-for-TV feel that makes it most suitable for middle-grade readers."

~ *Kirkus Review*

"**I LOVED IT**!! I was greatly **entertained** and impressed. The prose is quick, skillful, and **funny**, and the characterizations of the main figures are **vivid** without being overdrawn."

~ D. Patrick Miller, author of
How to Be Spiritual Without Being Religious

❧

"After reviewing the manuscript, I feel confident that **libraries would do well to have this book available** for their young patrons. In a world that seems to become more frightening by the day, this book is a call to action for young people to learn mindfulness skills as well as how to become more present in the moment, thus allowing them to gain an understanding of how to carry on no matter what their future holds. **Young readers will connect with both the human and animal characters** while learning about the ecosystems of the Everglades. This **story of interconnectedness** is a **timely topic**."

~ Grace Kastens, Public Library Director

❧

"The plot is **interesting** . . . The characters are **well drawn** . . . The dialog is very real, **very natural**, and in many places, **very funny** . . . The structure is **very good** . . . All in all, **very good work**."

~ Joanne Fowler, retired teacher

...TED
EVERGLADES
FRIEND FOR LIFE

G. A. KOWATCH

GREAT RAYS, LLC
Naples, Florida

Great Rays, LLC
2316 Pine Ridge Rd., #407, Naples, FL 34109
EnchantedEverglades.com

Wild animals are dangerous and should never be approached. Please visit the Everglades National Park's website for information on visitation rules, warnings, and more. NPS.gov/ever

Enchanted Everglades novel series is a fantasy—and, as such, the names, characters, and story events are products of the author's imagination. In addition, the ecosystems of the Everglades and Big Cypress National Park are condensed for dramatic effect.

Cover and Chapter Illustrations by Tim Shinn
Chapter Illustration Layout Designs by Anton Jaspard
Interior Layout Design by Victory Editing
Interior Layout by Victoria Vinton
Lotus (royalty-free image) © Gloria Rosazza | Dreamstime.com
Red Mangrove (royalty-free image) © 7active Studio | Dreamstime.com

Library of Congress Cataloging-in-Publication Data is available:
Library of Congress Control Number: 2019916127
ISBN 978-1-7335184-0-6 (hardcover)
ISBN 978-1-7335184-2-0 (paperback)
ISBN 978-1-7335184-1-3 (e-book)

Manufactured in the United States of America

*Dedicated to all the children
and animals of the world.*

CONTENTS

✿

Namaste
"The divine light in me bows to
the divine light in you."

✿

ONE

Goodbye

It is absolutely, positively true that a boy and a girl can be best friends, so long as they share similar interests and enjoy being together.

This was true of Ellen Hansen and me, best friends since the age of six without a single fight, not even over who'd get the last slice of veggie pizza. Friends had warned us that our friendship would never last. Too different, they said. Well, opposites attract, right?

Now as we celebrated Ellen's twelfth birthday at her house in Naples, Florida, a thunderstorm outside her bedroom window stomped the streets like a million marching hippos, but we didn't care. Ellen's dad was on his way home, and we were all going to the shelter to adopt a dog, one that Ellen and I could raise together. That was present number one.

While we waited, we read up on present number two: a weekend trip to the Everglades, a gift from my parents.

We'd already spent several hours talking about it, not to mention researching the ecosystems, the animals we'd see, even fables and legends like Yaha the ghost, who could talk to animals when he'd been alive.

Ellen's computer bleeped. "Ocean! An e-card from my dad!"

She clicked on the animated card, and Chihuahuas—with the faces of our parents, Ellen, and me—rapped a birthday song. We laughed, and to make Ellen laugh harder, I sang and danced along in a wacky way.

Once the video ended, Mr. Hansen appeared on the screen.

"Happy birthday, princess. I want to thank you for being the kindest and sweetest daughter ever. I'm so proud of you, and I look forward to all the wonderful things you'll do with your life. I sent this card so it'll arrive in your inbox at the same time I'll be home. See you soon, princess. Love you forever! Big kiss!"

I grinned. "Your dad's the best."

"He's my hero."

Before we could say anything else, we heard the strangest wail coming from Ellen's mom downstairs. It sounded like Hades was dragging her body into the underworld.

I held my breath, unsure of what to do. The only other sound was the rain pressure washing the windows.

"Ellen!" Mrs. Hansen cried out.

Rushing to get downstairs, Ellen knocked over her empty lemonade glass, which shattered on the floor. As I reached for the broken pieces, the pink desk lamp that

Mr. Hansen had given Ellen a few years ago flickered before turning off. I quickly dumped the shards of glass into the wastebasket and raced downstairs.

Maybe her mom had to throw away the birthday cake because she used salt instead of sugar. Maybe she smashed the cake on herself because a gnat surprised her by swooping up her nose. Or maybe she dropped the cake because a cockroach freaked her out by playing footsy with her toes. Three possibilities. Three things I'd done.

I found Ellen and her mom in the kitchen, holding each other tightly, their eyes closed.

A pink-and-white-frosted cake sat in the middle of the small table, and the smell of it filled the air. Pans and baking utensils waited in the sink. The only thing out of place was Mrs. Hansen's cell phone on the floor. I picked it up and placed it on the table.

"Hello. Is everything okay?" Obviously not. "Um, what happened?" Better question maybe.

Ellen stayed motionless, her eyes squeezed shut.

"Ocean," Mrs. Hansen said through her tears. "My husband was in a car crash." She sobbed. "He's gone."

What?

The rain stopped, and rays of light shone through the window.

I stared at the light as though it had slapped me. Did she mean he was dead?

I'd been with him and Ellen just yesterday, laughing at the video I'd put together for her birthday. No way he was *gone*.

"We have to go to the hospital mortuary and contact our family," she said. "Please go home and tell your parents. I'll phone them tomorrow."

"I'm . . . so sorry." I couldn't think clearly. Should I hug them?

"Bye, Ocean," Mrs. Hansen said.

"All right, bye." I stepped toward the door. "Ellen, I'll call you later?"

"Okay," she said without looking up.

I didn't know what else to do, so I rode my bike home. I felt empty, weird, as though a part of me had died and I hadn't said goodbye.

For the next five days, time didn't exist. Dates changed numbers, morning and night swapped places, and daily routines spun in a blur.

But today was the funeral, and time got unstuck.

Mom knocked on my bedroom door and came in. "Did you finish your sympathy card to Ellen?" She grabbed the yellow tie off my bed.

"Not yet. Did you send the flowers?" I slipped on my navy jacket.

"We delivered three beautiful vases to the church this morning." She wrapped the tie around my shirt collar and tied it for me, then tucked it all under my jacket.

"Nice, thanks."

"You doing okay?" She stroked my hair while her eyes misted. Mom had known tragedy. She'd tried to have babies, but they died before they were born. So they adopted me.

"Yeah, I'm okay." I hugged her, never wanting to see her hurt again.

The weird thing? I resembled my adoptive parents, except my eyes weren't green—they were closer to aqua blue. They'd thought the name Ocean was fitting and didn't think pairing it with the last name River was dumb, but the neighborhood bullies did. Ocean River. I liked it.

Dad poked his head into my bedroom. "How are you doing?"

I released Mom and shrugged. "Fine."

"It's not too late to cry," Dad said, walking in. "It's cleansing for the heart and mind."

These past few days Dad kept telling me to let it all out, but I couldn't cry. I couldn't feel anything. I couldn't believe I'd never see Mr. Hansen again. Saying goodbye at a funeral seemed unreal.

Mom said, "Come down when you're ready, darling." She and Dad left my room.

At my desk, I took out the photo album Ellen had given me for my twelfth birthday a month ago. Its photos spanned our six years of friendship from the first meeting at the Conservancy of Southwest Florida to the day she handed me this gift.

I smiled at the first page, where Ellen had written: *A shy girl met a quirky boy, and their lives changed forever.* I loved that.

As I thumbed through the album, searching for a photo to paste on the card, I found a silly picture of us when we were nine years old with our heads together, our eyes crossed, and our tongues out. I slipped that one into my wallet.

Eventually I found a picture of Ellen, her parents, and me using our fingers to lift the corners of our lips. Mr. Hansen would always do that to us whenever we looked sad, so I had started that joke in the picture.

I glued the photo on the outside of the card, and inside I wrote: *I'm so sorry he's gone. I've been thinking of you and your mom every day and praying that everyone is okay. I'm here for you always. Love, Ocean.*

I slid the card into my jacket pocket and stood up to stretch my tired body, still wobbly from lack of sleep.

As I headed down the four flights of stairs inside our sustainable tree house, I thought about Ellen.

We had chatted only briefly since her birthday. Her voice sounded the same way she'd been in the kitchen that day—lifeless, numb, and monotone. She didn't say much on the phone except that she was fine and busy with her relatives.

Mom told me to give her some healing time with her family. But I couldn't wait to see her.

I hoped the card would make her smile. If it didn't, I'd have to come up with another plan. Something hilarious, for sure.

TWO

Kill Time

It was a glorious winter afternoon at a pond in the Everglades, yet I couldn't enjoy it with my friends. Thoughts about the upcoming night consumed me.

Soon animals would sneak out from their dens, silently stalking through the ground or air. Built-in night goggles and other sensing abilities made them perfect hunters. Then violently they'd pounce on their prey, rip their flesh apart, and savagely eat. I didn't blame the carnivore animals. It was part of their design, part of nature's fragile balance. Regardless, my nerves would snap when I'd witness a killing.

I was an unusual alligator, and so predators wouldn't attack me, but that didn't matter. It also didn't matter that my father, the king of the Everglades, owned all the land. The only thing that mattered to me was to find somewhere safe for the night, free from slaughter. Our last site where we'd stayed safely for a few months had become a panther's hunting ground.

But what if we couldn't find a new place in time?

I exhaled deeply, trying to focus on my friends instead of my worries.

"Gumbo, there's some seaweed here you might like." Bix, a baby softshell turtle and one of my dear friends, beckoned me to join him.

"No thanks, Bix. I already had some cattails and pickerelweed." *Pickerelweed.* Whenever I ate that plant, whether or not its purple flowers had bloomed, I thought of Mother. *I'm so sorry. I'm sorry I couldn't save you. I miss you so much.*

Asha, a wood stork and my best friend, waltzed toward me from the pond's bank. Etched at the top of her walking stick was the *om* symbol. As she got closer, she shook her wet feathers, drenched earlier when she'd stepped into the depths.

Now inches from me, Asha gave me her unblinking stare, mentally communicating her message. She knew I was dwelling on the past again, thinking about Mother, which always hurt. So we crouched down to meditate, to clear our minds, to quiet our emotions, and to gain inner strength.

After twenty minutes, my breathing steadied and my core centered, so I chanted, "Om . . . Peace . . . Peace . . . Peace . . ."

"Planning on doing yoga, then hiding for the night?" The harsh voice splintering my calm energy came from my brother Cyp. He'd arrived with our other brother, Will, and one of their friends.

I recovered to set Bix on my shoulder and help Asha to her feet. We strolled away from the negative energy with our heads held high.

"While we hunt tonight," Cyp said, "Gumbo will scurry around like a tiny, frightened lizard, hiding from snakes and spiders."

"He's scared of critters?" Cyp's friend sounded shocked. Who wouldn't be?

Cyp laughed. "He's scared of anything that moves in the Everglades!"

"Yeah," Will said, "and he's friends only with animals we want to eat."

"I'm a strong leader, while Gumbo's a coward," Cyp bragged. "I'll make sure my father honors me as the junior king in a few months."

Cyp wanted the crown, and he could have it. Not a single alligator in the Everglades believed I could lead, and they were right.

"You'd be powerful, Cyp," Will said.

For some inexplicable reason, once we became teenagers a year ago, Will stopped hanging out with me and instead spent all his time with Cyp. I still wondered what had changed his mind.

"What about his golden eyes?" their friend asked. "And isn't Gumbo the eldest?"

"The golden eyes are a myth. He's neither the strongest nor the fastest alligator in the Everglades. I am!" Cyp yelled. "And who cares if he's older? We need a leader, not a yogi wannabe."

Now far enough away, I took in a deep, calming breath. I loved my brothers. I didn't want to fight them. Why couldn't they accept me for who I was?

My inner guide said, *Forgive everything*.

Every time someone hurt me, I forgave them.

"You haven't forgiven if you're still hurt," Asha said.

I'd previously thought she could read my mind, but the truth was, she just knew me too well.

I winked. "I'm a sensitive gator."

She let out her squawking laugh, and on cue, nearby trees rustled as birds fled her earsplitting voice. She stopped abruptly and faced me again.

"That you are. *If* you believe it." She flapped her damp wings to dry them further, then sniffed her feathers and shoved them against my nose. "Smell this."

"Excuse me?"

"Dead weasel? Deer dung?"

Sneezing, I patted the wings back against her sides. "You're fine, Asha."

"I think it smells like a rotten crawfish," Bix said.

He always made me smile.

Asha always made me grow spiritually. I took a moment to appreciate the intricate patterns and mesmerizing colors of her bald head and slender neck. How could anyone eat such an exquisite creature? If it weren't for Father's decree that alligators couldn't kill my friends, Cyp and Will would have devoured them long ago.

"Gumbo, you okay?" Bix tugged the mala beads around my neck.

"I'm fine," I said, not being perfectly honest. I wished Father would tell my brothers to quit bothering me. Instead, he'd just frown in my direction, expecting me to fight back. How could I stop them when the thought of bloodshed made me feel faint?

"Let's start looking for a calming space for the evening," I said.

Asha gave a single nod.

Bix hugged my neck. "It'll be quiet if you don't scream like you did last night."

I erased the terrible image of the panther killing the rabbit and concentrated on our search. We had only a few hours to find a secure place before nighttime. Before *kill time.*

THREE

The End

By the time we arrived at the church, the only seats left were in the back. In the front, Ellen and Mrs. Hansen sat in the left section, right corner, surrounded by their relatives. Standing flower sprays edged both ends. Below the altar in the middle, a ceramic urn rested on a pedestal next to three flower vases.

I quickly shifted my gaze to the right where a large photo of Mr. Hansen leaned against an easel next to more flowers. I wished he would show up and say this was all a joke—a really bad joke.

A woman spoke to the Hansens for a minute, then took her seat. I could do that too.

"Dad, can I give her my card now?"

"Just give it to her at the end."

"I'll be quick. I promise."

He checked his cell phone. "Okay, you have ten minutes before the service starts."

I rose and maneuvered through a minefield of knees and feet. Halfway along our row, I stepped on a man's giant black shoes. He jerked forward, bumping my head.

"Sorry!" I whispered.

I floundered for balance and grabbed a girl's blond ponytail.

"Ouch!" The girl pulled at her hair.

"Sorry!" Letting the hair go, I fell onto the lap of a heavyset woman who huffed and shooed me off. I stumbled out and made my way around the back of the nave, down the left aisle.

As I got closer to the front, I noticed Ellen wasn't crying. Everyone else appeared miserable except Ellen's grandfather, who sat there snoring.

Mr. Hansen wouldn't like all their unhappy faces.

A few years ago when my betta fish died, Mr. Hansen had said it was normal to feel sad, but after a while, I should move on and be happy because my fish had gone home to heaven. Ellen agreed with her dad, going on to decorate a small box for his coffin. She gave a heartfelt eulogy and reminded me how I saved his life when I'd found him thrown away in the trash. Afterward, both Ellen and Mr. Hansen made a point of spending time with me until I felt better.

Maybe there was something I could do now to make everyone feel happier.

Just as I was about to turn in to the Hansens' pew, a man and a woman cut in front of me. Not fair! I hurried behind the couple and searched for an opening between them, afraid I might lose my chance to speak to Ellen before the service started.

Not finding even the tiniest crack to squeeze through, I moved farther to the left of the couple. Then a little farther until suddenly, I found myself in the center aisle with everyone staring at me. I pulled the corners of my lips into a smile the way Mr. Hansen had always done. A few faces lit up, and some people nodded. When I wave-danced and jiggled my right leg, more people grinned, so that was good. I bet Mr. Hansen smiled from above. Then I saw my parents rise slightly from their seats, frowning and gesturing for me to stop, and that wasn't good.

As I was moving back toward the couple, I tripped on my loose shoelace, knocked against the pedestal—which landed with a *bang*—but I caught the urn! *Phew.*

Off-balance, I couldn't help tilting too far over the other way, shuffling straight for Mr. Hansen's photo. Someone shouted, "Oh no!" as I body-slammed the frame. It crashed to the floor. Glass cracked.

"Huh? What?" Ellen's grandfather barked as he woke up. "Where am I? Good thing I wore a diaper."

I stopped myself from stumbling onto the photo but leaned sideways too far and hobbled toward the flower arrangements. The first vase got kicked, the other two bumped and rolled. Water spilled. I began skating in place on the slippery floor. The urn escaped from my hands.

Mrs. Hansen cried out, "My Cuddle Cakes!"

I grabbed the urn again.

It slipped again.

"My Sugar Puff!"

I caught it and hugged it tight to my chest.

The skating stopped, but the wet marble floor made my feet spread, and I ended up in a split.

Whispers: "clumsy kid," "childish," "poor Mrs. Hansen," "feel so bad for them," echoed around the church. It went on and on, invisible arrows aimed straight to the bull's-eye: crazy, stupid me.

I set the urn down and managed to push myself up. Right away I glanced at Ellen. With her arms pressed tight to her sides, her eyebrows squished together, and her eyes and lips mere slits—she was furious.

"Sorry," I mumbled.

Ellen continued to scowl while Mrs. Hansen took in the destruction, hands to her face, head shaking.

Totally embarrassed, I hurried out the nearest wooden doors, shoelace flapping on the marble floor.

On the steps outside, I replayed the disaster in my head. I'd goofed up big time. Super big. I'd ruined events in the past but never something this important. Why couldn't I have been more careful, more patient? If I'd waited to give Ellen my card *after* the service as Dad had suggested, none of this would have happened.

How I wished I could go back in time for a do-over!

Behind me, the door opened.

Ellen.

"I'm so sorry. My shoelace. I—"

"You're too immature to be my friend anymore." Her tears were flowing now. "You know how much I loved him. How much I'll miss him. Yet you turned his funeral into a joke like you do with everything. Just stay away from me!" She stormed back inside.

Seeing her cry, it finally hit me. Mr. Hansen was dead. The nice man who had been so kind, so funny, so full of life and wisdom, was really gone. Poof! Just like that. We would never, ever see him again for the rest of our lives.

Like one of those babies who couldn't get their wails out fast enough, I hiccup-cried. My parents rushed out of the church and practically carried me to the car. I knew they'd lecture me tomorrow, though not now while I was hurting.

After Dad took the wheel, I got in the front by Mom, hoping she'd console me. They both kept saying things like, "It'll be okay. Mr. Hansen is in heaven with God." And "Don't worry, I'm sure the Hansens will forgive you." It didn't help. I couldn't stop crying. It was the end of Mr. Hansen.

Eventually Mom cried too, which only made me cry harder. Dad tried to soothe her, but his mouth quivered funny as if his lips tickled, then he joined in the cryfest.

Mom and I stopped for a second to watch him because he sounded so much like a roaring bear. And he kept nodding and saying, "It's cleansing. It's cleansing."

FOUR

Swamp Thingy

Asha, Bix, and I hiked deeper into the swamp, admiring the cypress trees with their buttressed trunks often six feet wide. Their roots, called cypress knees, stuck out of the water, surrounding them like an army on guard. Red epiphytes burrowed in the trees' every nook, adding color to the brown-and-green landscape.

Standing upright for a better vantage point, I inspected the clear, shallow water. Finding nothing, I searched for cozy places to sleep. Just beyond us, next to the cypress swamp, an area appeared to be safe and quiet. I meditated on that choice for a moment.

"Om—" Wait. I sensed something watching us. "Hold on, Asha."

I scanned the perimeter. I sniffed the windless air. Many animals hid nearby: a fox squirrel, a barn owl, a leopard frog, a tricolored heron, and—a Burmese python! Where was he? I checked the ground, the trees, the shrubs—

The soft rustling of ferns spiked my adrenaline.

Next to a tree, beneath overhanging coco plums, a single dying fern swayed above the dense shadows. I held my breath, waiting nervously for signs of activity. Asha cocked her head that way. Bix scratched and smelled an armpit, oblivious to my apprehension.

Should we get away now?

Something slithered out from the camouflage of dead ferns. A sinister smile stretched across his enormous face, almost splitting it in two.

"We should run," Asha said rather calmly.

Holding on to Bix, I grabbed Asha and splashed through the wetland in the opposite direction. I glanced over my shoulder and found that *swamp thingy* chasing us!

Incredibly faster and larger than a regular Burmese python, he could easily swallow all three of us in one bone-crunching gulp.

My inner guide said, *Do not feed fear with more negativity and doubt.*

But I couldn't help myself. With every second, panic mounted.

The thrashing behind me edged closer, and my muscles surged with energy. I started to hyperventilate.

The python grunted, moving faster.

Asha tilted her head and stared off to one side as if mentally conversing with spirits. "Turn right," she said.

I followed her direction, raced a few more yards, and found safety. In the sawgrass marsh clearing, cordoned off by Father's tough military officers, thirty or more soldiers were exercising.

Normally you'd find me far from their training ground, but now they were a blessing. A godsend even.

"Namaste," I said. "Would it be okay to watch for a few minutes?"

"Sure," the drill sergeant said. "Anything for the king's eldest son."

The soldiers doing push-ups drooled over Asha; at least they ignored Bix.

As I stood beside the sergeant, I searched for the python and found him forty feet away, ensconced in a thicket, eyes glinting. A few minutes later, he swung his head around and disappeared.

I exhaled with profound gratitude and inhaled with intense nausea at the thought of almost being eaten. I'd never seen anything like that monster. He would have killed us if I hadn't gone the right way. Just the thought of that thing hiding in the bushes, ready to spring out, ready to attack, made me sick.

"You're embarrassing yourselves, Privates! I want to see double time! Now!"

"Yes, sir! Yes, sir!"

"Thank you, Sergeant." I grabbed Asha and set off.

Once we were far enough away, and when I couldn't hold it any longer, I threw up near a shrub.

Bix slipped down my shoulder and into the dark green pool at my feet. He stretched his arms and rubbed it all over himself.

He beamed. "Nice. The acid cleaned all the crud off me and in places I couldn't reach. Thanks!"

I covered my mouth. That didn't stop the projectile vomit from gushing through my fingers.

FIVE

Without Me

After wrecking Mr. Hansen's funeral, I got angry at God and even begged him to bring Mr. Hansen back. But it was hopeless. I felt as if plastic food wrap covered me like an unwanted leftover.

"Clinically depressed," the doctor said.

I stayed in bed all day under the covers, avoiding everyone. I didn't read a book or go outside or play with our pets. Xela, our AI, tried to cheer me up with more than a hundred jokes. None worked, so I blocked her from my bedroom and terrace for being annoying. I knew Mr. Hansen wouldn't like me staying sad, but I still couldn't shake off the heaviness.

Eventually my parents and friends poked holes in the plastic of the depression, then ripped it apart. They forced me to spend time in nature and with animals, to volunteer at a foundation, to exercise at our gym, and to take extra vitamins and minerals. All good stuff. Even though I got better because of their efforts, as long as I didn't hear from Ellen, I couldn't feel happy. Maybe after some time passed, she and I could be friends again. Or so my parents promised.

After a couple of weeks, I called Ellen's house and got Mrs. Hansen.

"It's okay, Ocean. It was just an accident. Of course we forgive you. What's over is over."

She said *we*. Did that mean Ellen felt the same?

"Is Ellen available to talk?"

There was a brief pause, then dead air. She came back on and said, "I'm sorry, Ocean, she's ironing clothes. She'll call you when she's free."

"Okay. Please tell her I'm really sorry."

"I will, Ocean. Goodbye."

The call never came.

A few weeks later, I rode my bike to Ellen's. As I held Mom's gift—raw spirulina cookies—I wondered if Ellen was still mad at me. I hadn't seen her since the funeral and didn't know what to expect.

Mrs. Hansen opened the door. "Hi, Ocean, how are you doing?"

I almost didn't recognize her. She looked like she hadn't eaten for weeks and had binge-watched her favorite show without sleeping.

"I'm fine. I'm sorry again, Mrs. Hansen."

"You don't have to keep apologizing. Come on in. It's nice to see you."

She gave me a sympathetic look, and I returned one of my own. It must have been really hard for her.

"May I see Ellen? I brought her favorite cookies."

"She's cleaning the bathroom right now, and I know

she's swamped with homework. But I'll see if she can stop for a minute." She moved to the stairs. "*Nena*. Ocean is here. Can you come down for a few minutes, please?"

When no response came, she went upstairs.

The house—tidy except for the dining room table, which held a laptop and stacks of paper—felt empty without Mr. Hansen. He'd laughed a lot, the sound booming throughout the house. I could almost see the family playing video games together.

Upstairs, faint conversation turned into hushed arguing. That could only mean one thing: Ellen didn't want to see me. Why couldn't she say hello for one second? Was I that horrible?

Mrs. Hansen came back downstairs, not looking directly at me. "Sorry, Ocean. She's up to her arms with cleanser, then it's homework. Poor Ellen works like a horse doing all the chores around the house since I've had to take on two jobs. Come back another time?"

"Okay. Could you please give her these cookies and let her know I'm here for her?" I didn't say another word. I couldn't let her see me cry.

"I will. Thank you, Ocean. That was thoughtful of you and your mom. See you soon."

After trying a few more times to see Ellen, I gave up. She couldn't or wouldn't see me. Mom told me that every single person reacts differently to trauma and stress. She said to forget her for now and focus on my studies. Though as hard as I tried, I couldn't get her out of my mind.

In the spring, two months after the funeral fiasco with zero contact from Ellen, my parents thought it was the perfect time for Ellen's belated gift: the weekend trip to the Everglades.

I didn't want to go. I bet Ellen didn't want to go. Unfortunately, we both had to go.

We were also celebrating Mrs. Hansen's new job at L.O. Industries, a big corporation. Dad had set up the interview because he knew them. He'd sold some top secret inventions to that business. For some reason, Mom didn't like that company, but she was glad Mrs. Hansen had a higher-paying job.

Just then, we pulled up to Ellen's home, and my heart performed plyometric jumps.

Mrs. Hansen waved and smiled as she came out while Ellen frowned slightly.

Yep. She didn't want to be here.

After Dad put their bags in the trunk, Mrs. Hansen opened the car door and said hello to Mom. She also nudged—maybe pushed—Ellen to sit in the middle next to me while she sat by the window.

"Hi, Mrs. Hansen. Hi, Ellen," I said.

"Hi everyone," Ellen mumbled, not looking at me. She made sure our legs didn't touch.

Fine by me!

"Hello, Ocean. This tiny puppy is Nano, Ellen's new rescue. Isn't he cute as a ribbon?" Mrs. Hansen rubbed the little head of a Chihuahua mix sitting on Ellen's lap. His straggly yet puffy white hair wiggled.

Nano wasn't one of the three small dogs we'd selected as a possibility on her birthday. She must have picked him up recently—without me.

As I stared out the side window, I wished I had wings. It must be nice to be a bird able to soar through the skies and go wherever you want.

I loved the birds, squirrels, and rabbits that visited my feeder as much as I loved my family's rescue animals—all being spoiled by my grandparents this weekend—but I'd been looking forward to raising a dog with Ellen.

These new emotions stirring up inside me were confusing. All I knew was that I hurt. I thought she knew me. I'd done crazy stunts in the past, all meant to be funny, or sometimes I'd messed up, like three years ago when I dropped her birthday cake on myself and fell on her presents. She forgave me. Why not now? I bet she never saw me—the real me.

Maybe having the same interests didn't matter, or maybe she just didn't like being with me anymore.

I tuned out of the scene, though I kept one ear alert for any conversation about Ellen.

After driving for an hour on US 41, we were almost at the tour. Our moms had chatted about all kinds of stuff. They spoke mostly about their work. Mom mentioned that I'd jumped another semester in homeschooling. Dad revealed that I wrote songs of "love and heartbreak" for my band, which got him a glare from me. Why did he have to say that?

According to Mrs. Hansen, Ellen barely had time for schoolwork yet still made the honor roll. Not a surprise. She was smart.

I unwrapped a raw nut bar and bit into it. Mom had given us a handful in case we got hungry between meals during the weekend.

An ibis skimmed next to my window, ogling my snack. Cool. I recognized the curved orange beak on the white body. They'd come to our yard at home, eating all the grubs, acting as natural pesticides.

I slowly ate the last piece, and his eyes popped.

Slap! The ibis hit a PANTHER CROSSING sign.

I glanced back to see if he was okay, but we were too far gone. When I twisted back around, I accidentally bumped into Ellen, knocking her feet from the center floor hump.

"Oops, sorry," I said and grabbed Nano before he fell.

His tiny, soft body smelled of baby shampoo. Before I could pet his cute round forehead, Ellen reached for him, and when her hands brushed against mine, I let him go. I felt shy for some reason. Even frowning, she looked pretty in a ponytail, dressed in her jeans, T-shirt, and khaki jacket.

Mom had made me a blue shirt using Dad's 3D printer. "To bring out your gorgeous eyes," she'd said. Yeah, I knew she was trying to make me feel confident. But then she also printed me sneakers with hook-and-loop fastener tabs—no more tripping on shoelaces for me. That was a big hint. I hadn't worn sneakers like that since I was four.

Ellen leaned forward. "Mr. and Mrs. River, could we just skip the tour and go to Everglades City? We're not prepared if something goes wrong on the airboat."

She clutched her mom's hand and hugged Nano with her other arm. Her dad's accident must have made her more cautious and worried.

Imitating a trailer from a horror movie, sound effects included, I said, "*Braaam . . . Braaam . . .* From the producers who brought you *Sweaty Eyebrows* and the *Googly Eyes Are Watching* trilogy comes an adventure into the dark and scary world of giant pythons. *Braaam . . .* Angry gators. *Braaam . . .* Hungry panthers—"

"Ocean."

Mom had a hundred ways to say my name, and I knew the meaning of each one.

"Don't worry, be joyful," Mrs. Hansen said.

Don't worry, be happy? For some reason, Mom's left eye would twitch every time Mrs. Hansen changed a cliché.

"We'll be okay. It's just a short, thirty-minute ride," Dad said. "Early tomorrow morning we'll head back here from the hotel for a swamp walk, then a nature hike through the woods before we take a buggy to the campground and stay overnight. The next day, we're set to go boating. It'll be fun."

I smiled at Ellen and Nano. "That sounds like a blast."

Ellen's frown eased a tiny bit. Nano buried his face in Ellen's belly. Even if the weekend didn't make us friends again, we should definitely have a great time.

My parents had planned everything perfectly except Dad thought Mom had made the reservation for the airboat tour. Since Dad called last minute, all the tours were fully booked, but one place was willing to take us on a private airboat ride. After that, we'd still have enough time to visit Everglades City before having dinner at a nearby restaurant and checking in to the hotel.

"Bet your bottom penny we'll have the best time," Mrs. Hansen said.

Mom's eye twitched again.

We slowed behind a large beige car traveling at twenty miles an hour in a fifty-five zone. Its right turn signal blinked continuously, pointing toward the swamp.

Dad sped into the left lane to pass. In the car was an elderly couple, so short we could barely see more than the tops of their heads. The man wore an old-style hat; the woman, a gray Halloweenish wig. From the front of their car, I couldn't see anyone. It was as if ghosts were driving the car. Too funny.

"There's the Lady Airboat Tours!" Mom yelled, making us jump.

Dad swerved into the tour's parking lot, nearly killing a crow pecking on the ground. The crow fled to a tree where he perched and cawed loudly at us. I wasn't sure if he was telling us off or warning us not to go on the tour.

SIX

Sheer Luck

Next to a small tree island at a vacant gator hole ten feet in diameter, Asha, Bix, and I arrived for a meal. The sweet smell of wildflowers and the warmth of the sun invited us in. I reached for the cattails and gorged.

Two months had passed since we'd narrowly escaped the mutant python. I hadn't seen him again though I dreamed of him chasing me almost every night. I had tried everything from meditation to positive affirmations to calm my nerves, yet nothing could ease my tension.

Asha tried to help me. She said, "The cure is within."

If I could heal myself of anxiety, I would have done it years ago.

As a last resort, I visited the bobcat psychiatrist who asked me to come back in a few days for alternative treatments using neurolinguistic programming, tapping, and hypnosis. In the meantime, she told me not to get stressed.

That wasn't possible, at least not on this day.

Father had called a special meeting. All the tribal chiefs had to be there, which meant it was serious business.

Just the idea of facing all those leaders jangled my nerves.

At the end of every meeting in the past, Cyp had told a derogatory joke at my expense. Everyone laughed, of course. I was the odd son, the spiritual crazy. I didn't fit in with any tribe, not even with my own family.

Cyp had also spread a hurtful rumor that I wasn't his brother and that our parents had found me in a human tourist site, dressed in a tutu. That joke led to endless gibes and tree carvings of me dancing in ballet costumes. I didn't want to face more of that today.

I brainstormed excuses to avoid the meeting. An upset stomach, my favorite, came close to being accurate, but I'd overused that.

Asha searched the shallow fringe of the gator hole and clamped her bill around a prized crayfish.

Bix emerged from the water smiling wide, as always.

"You okay, Gumbo?" Bix asked.

"I'm fine." I sighed deeply. "Truth be told, I'm not feeling centered. I don't want to go to the meeting because they all think I'm a loser and Cyp is going to embarrass me again."

"The only gator you need to please is yourself," Asha said. "But you have to go. The officer said you had to be there—a direct order from the king."

"Why do I have to go? Father knows I'm not going to follow through with any command unless it's nonviolent. Why can't we have prayer circles and positive-intention meditations?"

"I like it," Bix said. "All those gators stare at me and lick their lips. They want to be my friend."

"Bix, they want to . . . Uh, never mind."

"If you don't go, I'll scream," Asha said.

No, not her screams. The sound could split old trees in two. Alligators miles away would hear it, and Father would have them drag me to the meeting anyway.

"I guess it doesn't matter. I'll always be a coward."

"No way! You're my hero!" Bix said. "I'm alive because of you."

Before I could answer him, an eastern indigo snake slithered near me, and I reacted on impulse, splashing into the gator hole. I resurfaced and searched for the snake.

"It was sheer luck. Right place at the right time," I said.

A year ago, when Bix had swum out of a gator hole much like this one, an alligator snuck up from the water. Behind a wall of trees, Asha had been showing me the locust pose. I tried it and flipped my back too far, knocking a palm tree off its roots. The tree tumbled on the alligator, thereby saving Bix. That wasn't bravery.

"We are here to save each other," Asha said. On her forehead was a fishing spider, glaring at me for being catapulted out of the water when I'd jumped in.

I leaped straight out of the gator hole in a fierce yoga pose, drenching Asha again. The spider sprang off her and dove back in.

"Blessings! Love and light!" I prayed he didn't come back.

Asha opened her left wing where a thick purple scar trailed through her scapula and joints. "You saved us that day. I am forever grateful, my brother." Asha joined her wing tips together in a prayer position and bowed.

When I first met Asha a couple of years ago, she and her parents had been practicing transcendental meditation next to a pond.

Out of nowhere, a mature black bear stood on his hind legs and roared. Asha fiercely protected her parents by standing in front of them. Sadly the bear slashed her left wing, forever damaging it. Just then I surged straight out of the water, double the bear's height, and apparently I scared him because he fled on all fours. I apologized profusely, not knowing I'd saved their lives.

"Again, sheer luck," I said and bowed. Asha bowed. I bowed. She bowed. I bowed.

"That's enough." Asha tapped my face and tried to pinch my bony cheeks. "You're too cute."

"I miss your parents," I said. "They were enlightened teachers." They had died last year from toxic green algae.

"Just talk to them. The first words and answers you hear from your mind are them."

A crayfish by her foot covered his ears. She picked him up with her bill and gave him to Bix, who decided to play with him.

"Time for the meeting," Asha said and marched ahead.

"Wait." I ransacked my brain for ideas while I scooped up Bix.

Asha stopped. "Don't make me carry you."

"You can tell them I have to save the owner of the gator hole."

"Really," Asha said, then pointed to a corner. "The owner just woke up."

"Someone's voice is too loud," said a stout alligator sliding out of his den and rubbing his eyes. "Hey, what are you doing in my home?" He charged toward me.

I grabbed Asha and sprinted off before his crooked teeth could catch my tail.

"Thanks for the cattails!" I sped toward the dreaded meeting.

On the way, I chanted affirmations I'd learned from Asha. *I am divine. I am eternal. I am a spirit, not a body. I am perfect as God created me. No words can hurt me.* Saying those phrases usually gave me strength, though not this time. Something inside was stronger. Was it the ego? Self-hate? Fear? Intuition? I didn't know. But my body knew, and it responded with frazzled nerves.

SEVEN

Shady Tour

At the tour, only one other car was in the lot: a blue Mustang with massive tires and caked-on mud decorating the wheels' edges. A warning written on duct tape—DON'T YOU TOUCH MY CAR—stretched across a broken window.

There were two one-story wooden buildings, once painted red and gray but now weather faded. One door led to a souvenir store. Alligator heads with creepy glass eyes twinkled through the window. Who'd want to buy that?

In the smaller building—a ticket booth—a shadowy figure moved across the tinted glass, and the OPEN sign flipped to CLOSED. A thin dude strutted out the door. He wore a camo T-shirt with a matching hat.

"Can't wait for them pitchers of beer and fried frog legs," he said, talking on his cell phone.

Frog legs? Gross. Dad had said they tasted like chicken, but as a vegetarian, I had no clue what chicken tasted like.

The dude slipped his phone into his baggy jeans and saw us. "You the Rivers?"

Dad answered, "Yes."

"Well, it's about time. If you folks hadn't of made it, you'd be out of luck 'cause we'll be closed tomorrow for a funeral." With a gleam in his beady eyes, he added, "Owner's husband is headin' to the Dirt Motel." He pressed his thin lips firmly together as if trying not to laugh at his own joke. Not pretty.

"My name's Dale, and the kids can call me Mr. Dale. We better get goin', but I need to see the cash."

Mr. Dale's eyes lit up when Dad handed over the money. He took it and ran to a small gray airboat instead of the big red ones near the ticket booth.

Mom frowned, and I knew exactly why. Her conspiracy radar was beeping. *Beep, beep, beep.*

"Shouldn't he be putting the money in the office?" Mom asked. "Are you sure he's one of the drivers?"

"It'll be fine, honey. It's only for thirty minutes."

Dad had every right to be confident. As a scientist and inventor, he could fix and build anything. Though Mom's instincts were always right, and that worried me. I hoped this wasn't a shady tour. I didn't want anything to go wrong on this trip. The Hansens needed some fun, not more tragedy.

Carrying my waist pack stuffed with the raw bars and my wallet, I circled around the car to where Mrs. Hansen and Ellen had gotten out.

"Need any help?" I asked Mrs. Hansen and Ellen.

"No, thanks," Ellen said. She reached into the back seat for her mom's jacket and handed it to her. "It might get cold later. Do you have your water? Cell phone? Bug spray? Snacks?"

Ellen and her lists. List of things to do. List of things to eat. List of things to list. There was nothing wrong with that, but I bet she had a list of pros and cons for our friendship—and cons won, for sure.

Mrs. Hansen patted Ellen's shoulder. "If I missed anything, I'll walk the bridge when I come to it." She held Nano so Ellen could wear the dog carrier she'd made the day before Mr. Hansen died.

Ellen gently touched the Miami blue butterfly patches stitched on the front, probably remembering how Mr. Hansen had said he loved the carrier, especially these endangered butterflies. Once Ellen put it over her head, Mrs. Hansen placed the little pup inside. Funny how he was still too small for it.

"Speed it up, kids," Mrs. Hansen said and left.

I wrapped my hiking pack around my waist, the water canister attached to one end.

"How have you been?" I asked.

"Fine. And you?"

"Fine. Sorry about everything."

"It doesn't matter." She moved faster to finish buckling the dog carrier.

It doesn't matter because there was nothing to forgive or because she was brushing me off?

Various mosquitoes swarmed us, some fast and almost invisible. Bigger ones hovered in slow motion, looking like miniature pterodactyls.

I swatted the mosquitoes as part of a dance to make it more fun. I slapped my left thigh, slapped my right thigh, slapped my left arm, slapped my right arm. Then I clapped the air above my head to be silly. Any chance that made Ellen smile?

Her back was to me. Did she turn away when I'd danced?

She closed the car door, then tapped her water canister, various objects inside her pockets, and Nano's head, as if checking off a list.

"You may want to hold the little guy tight," I told her, "so he doesn't fall into the water."

She knew alligators snacked on little animals such as dogs, so I was surprised Nano had come along. The idea of a hungry gator jumping toward Ellen to get at a meal made me nervous.

I yanked the carrier strap at her back. "You know alligators—"

She sprinted toward the others.

Did she think I'd mess things up? Make her lose Nano? Even though I didn't expect to be best friends again, I thought we could be regular friends.

I dug into my waist pack and removed the photo of Ellen and me from my wallet. Just as I was about to rip the thing, a clanking to my left stopped me.

With his head trapped inside a white plastic bag, a brown pelican wobbled, then bumped into a trash can. I stuffed the photo into my left pants pocket and headed toward him.

The car locked with a *beep*. I glanced over at the airboat, and Dad waved at me to hurry.

"Be right there!" I waved back.

I tiptoed toward the pelican. "It's okay. I won't hurt you. Let me help you."

He stopped moving, unable to see through the plastic, yet he seemed to trust me. I peeled the bag away from his head. *Pee-ew.* He reeked of dead fish. A jagged scar circled his beak, as though a large can had been stuck there before.

"Are you okay?"

He bent his head as if answering yes, then flew toward the airboat and parked on the dock post.

Before heading to the boat, I threw the bag into the overflowing trash can. On my way, the mosquitoes joined me, so I did the mosquito dance again. The pelican stared while Ellen shook her head.

Abruptly I stopped clowning. My silly dances used to make Ellen giggle, but now I was afraid they only reminded her of the funeral.

Once I got on the airboat, the hot metal seat toasted my buns in the second row with my parents, behind Ellen and her mom. Old and shabby, the boat didn't have guardrails, and a white bucket in the corner had flies and gnats in a frenzy over what looked like pink juice and chicken skin. Were they feeding chickens to gators in exchange for a show? Probably.

The pelican hopped to the front of the airboat and imitated my mosquito dance. So cool!

"That's my dance!" I jumped up to show Mom.

She took a cell phone video of me and the pelican dancing.

A year ago, Dad told me Mom had always wanted to take dance classes with her daughter and was sad she never got the chance. When I'd found Mom in the kitchen, I hugged her and told her I would take classes with her. We practiced a few hours a week, which I enjoyed because my funny variations made her laugh.

Mr. Dale handed out gobs of cotton to stuff our ears.

Mom removed the section that Mr. Dale had touched. She had cancer before, so she was careful about anything that'd lower her immune system such as germs.

"An airboat's decibels are between eighty and ninety," Dad said, wearing his scientist hat. "It can cause hearing damage without proper earmuffs. This may not be adequate protection."

"What?" Mr. Dale stuck a finger in his right ear and jiggled it.

Nano peeked above Ellen's shoulders, making eye contact with Mr. Dale.

"We ain't allowed to bring them dogs in airboats and trails. Gators can smell dander. They like them tasty little meat." Mr. Dale licked his lips. "In barbecue sauce."

Nano disappeared inside the pouch.

Poor Nano. He might become barbecue alongside them frog legs.

"Alligators aren't going to attack us, are they?" Dad asked.

"Well, no, it ain't the norm unless they got a nest they protectin' or got aggressive from people feedin' them or got real hungry." Mr. Dale laughed, showing a mouthful of rotten teeth.

He instantly became my inspiration to never, ever complain about brushing and flossing.

"I'll let that one slide if you pay me more money."

"That's fine. I'll pay you at the end of the tour," Dad said.

The pelican flew away when the engine started. Mr. Dale stepped on the accelerator. Nothing. He stomped it. Still nothing. That wasn't good. He pounded hard a few more times, and finally the airboat revved up. Mom gave me tissues to cover my nose from the exhaust fumes.

Mr. Dale shifted the rudder stick, and the airboat blared down the waterway, pushing spatterdock and lilies against the tall trees lining both sides. And yeah, I could still hear it loudly through the flimsy cotton in my ears.

The boat raced at a wacko speed. Sure, it was fun, though it couldn't be good. For one thing, plants got pummeled. And for another, what if he hit a bump or swerved too fast? On internet videos, airboats raced at over fifty miles per hour, and they seemed safe, so I might be overreacting. But maybe I wasn't. I didn't trust Mr. Dale, so I held on to my seat.

We were in for either an exciting adventure or a colossal disaster.

EIGHT

A Winner

In the cypress dome, more than a hundred alligators from several tribes lay in the pond, facing us. Elevated on a mound, Father stood in the center, Will and Cyp to his left and Asha and me to his right. Bix sprawled on my shoulder, waving to gators.

Father had ruled for many years with Mother, keeping the peace among the tribes and between the other animals in the Everglades, yet he hadn't kept the peace among his three sons.

In the last meeting months ago, when Father had said that an oil leak had caused irreparable damage to the environment, animals, and humans, Cyp had chimed in, "Just look at Gumbo. He's proof of damage!"

Father's stern gaze said it all. While he respected Cyp's military prowess, he wasn't proud of his bullying. At least we had that in common.

"Good afternoon," Father said to the noisy crowd to start the meeting.

He discussed many issues facing the Everglades, such as deadly pollution from human pesticides and rising water levels from global warming. I feared Father would mention the pythons and command us to kill them all, but thankfully, he didn't.

Several tribal leaders asked for advice, and Father handled them well. His answers benefited all parties so that no one lost. He was a fearless leader; I was not. Hearing all the problems and complaints agitated me.

I turned my attention to the pond's outer rim, where cypress trees with a canopy of ferns protected foot-long gators playing with their moms.

Gumbo, come here my little darling and give me a kiss.

Mother would ask me that several times a day. Then I'd jump up on her and plant the noisiest kisses on her face.

Asha glanced at me, recognizing that I'd drifted into a memory clip of Mother. I nodded and took a deep breath.

Be present. Be here.

I chanted quietly, using the mala beads on my wrist to keep calm and focused on the *now.*

"The exotic pythons are eating all the animals and disrupting the ecosystem!" Father yelled.

There. He mentioned them.

Did he know about the mutant python, more than thirty feet long, prowling in the Everglades?

The tribal leaders swished their tails and shouted, "Kill them!"

"We don't know where they came from," Father said. "But they have to be eliminated, one hundred percent."

A louder reaction discharged from the group, echoing through the dome, making me cringe.

"By tomorrow, all of you must report back with at least one dead python," Father ordered. "Awards will be given to those who kill the most and those who kill the largest."

Once the meeting ended, I chanted faster.

"Gumbo will win both awards," Cyp sneered.

Everyone bellowed with laughter except Father. I expected the dig, yet it still hurt. Being mocked repeatedly didn't desensitize me. I never got used to it, and because I couldn't stop it, it hurt me more each time.

"Yes, he will win both awards," Father said. "Gumbo *is* a winner."

The cypress dome fell silent.

NINE

Eeny, Meeny, Miny, Moe

The airboat sped between tree islands and sawgrass that framed the waterway. A small flock of American coots jetted over us. Mr. Dale whisked the boat sharply to chase after them, probably dreaming of ducks on the grill.

We passed a signpost to our right that I couldn't read, partly because water had splashed into my eyes and partly because branches covered some of the words. I hoped it wasn't important. My parents didn't seem to notice, so it must have been nothing.

About ten minutes later, we slowed near a maze of tree islands, and Mr. Dale shut the engine off.

"Them there wadin' birds is white egrets. That there with the poofy feathers is a snowy white egret."

Our moms snapped photos just before the egrets flew away. I'd run away too if I were an egret. Even though we didn't see many animals or birds, being outdoors was always awesome—and healthy, according to Mom.

"Up there . . . uh . . . a hawk," Mr. Dale said.

"That's an osprey," I told my parents.

"Did know. I ain't stupid." Mr. Dale's lips curled.

Nano whimpered.

"What's wrong, baby?" Ellen asked. She followed Nano's gaze to a pond apple tree.

Mr. Dale grinned. "Maybe he'd seen that ghost Yaha, looking for his lady love, Eleanor. Poor dude lost her after they eloped back in them early days. She was a white Christian missionary, and he was a Seminole Indian."

A book about Everglades fables and legends showed Yaha with shoulder-length hair, wearing a printed tunic over baggy pants. I studied the pond apple tree but didn't see a ghostly figure.

Yaha supposedly gave lost kids in the Everglades the temporary ability to talk to all kinds of creatures. Another book stated that Yaha could shape-shift into living things. For Ellen and me, his superpowers sounded ideal and a lot of fun.

Ellen glanced at me, and I shrugged.

On the same tree, a tiny lizard called a green anole skipped to the end of a branch and stared at Ellen. To get her attention, he bobbed rapidly, then swung his red dewlap, striking against his green skin. Ellen didn't notice or care.

I waved to him. He ignored me until I showed him a nut bar. He bobbed again and gave me the dewlap to ask for food. Then he looked back at Ellen, then again at me.

Mr. Dale started the airboat and took off at the same wacko pace as before.

When I waved goodbye to the anole, I thought he waved back.

I glanced over at Dad, punching numbers or notes into his cell phone, not paying attention to Mr. Dale or the tour. I wished he wasn't a workaholic. Mom said he worked hard to make sure we had everything because he'd been poor growing up. That was fine and all, but I'd rather see more of him than be rich.

Mom worked a lot too, selling her raw vegan food products and health stuff, though she would spend many hours each day homeschooling me. A couple of days a week, she also practiced yoga and meditation with her friends. Dad said meditation helped her when she'd lost her babies. And I'd only learned about her cancer a few years ago after she'd already healed.

I peered at her now, her arm wrapped around my shoulders. She kissed my forehead. I loved her so much.

Once we reached an area of towering trees and winding waterways, Mr. Dale twirled the airboat in wide circles, as if confused.

I knew we could backtrack, but after spinning several times, I couldn't tell which direction we'd come from. And from the puzzled look on Mr. Dale's face, he didn't know either.

"We need to be heading back," Dad said.

"I'm taking y'all on the scenic route." Mr. Dale laughed nervously while swatting at horseflies. "Anyway, we got seventy-two hours to get back before we's all jerky treats for them turkey vultures." He stared at Ellen and me. "Forty-eight for you kids."

Dad frowned. "In three and a half hours, it'll be dark."

"Hold on ta yer designer pants, mister. We goin' back now. Don't you worry. I know the way."

Over her shoulder, Ellen gave Mr. Dale a peeved expression.

Mrs. Hansen and Mom checked their cell phones and shook their heads.

Dad checked his phone. "No bars, honey. But getting lost without phone service has given me several ideas for apps." He started typing into his phone.

The seventy-two-hour or forty-eight-hour deadline might be the worst-case scenario when people lost in the woods ran out of clean water and died. Now I wished I'd studied wilderness survival techniques, at least the basics of how to start a fire, how to make a shelter, how to collect food and water, and how to protect myself. I knew a few things. Like zero.

Maybe fifteen minutes later, we entered narrow channels where tall trees blotted out most of the light, and the air felt denser, cooler, and stagnant. Once we got farther into the winding swamp forest, the scent of decaying plant matter, mixed with sweet and sour greenery, itched my nose. Mosquitoes and other flying bugs hovered and zigzagged through the air, biting us relentlessly. Mrs. Hansen shared her bug spray and gave us disposable bug wipes for later. Mom had forgotten her citronella oil.

On my right side, I recognized the cypress trees. Wait, what? I leaned forward. Gators! Hundreds of gators! What were they all doing? Having a meeting? It sure looked like it. Four tall and bulky alligators stood upright at the center like they were the leaders. How could they stand like that?

"Hey, look at all those gators," I said. But the airboat pushed into a different channel, moving away from the strange gathering. So much for that. Seeing a gator—seeing dozens—was cool, though I was glad we weren't any closer. The thought of all those alligators attacking this little boat scared me.

We slowed in front of several channels. Mr. Dale mouthed the words *eeny, meeny, miny, moe* while pointing, then turned the airboat toward *moe*. Unreal. Yep, we were lost for sure, and no matter how hard I tried to convince myself otherwise, the next few hours could be our last. Dramatic, I know. But hey, it could be true.

TEN

Python Challenge

When Father had said that I would win both awards and that I was a winner, his piercing gaze latched on to mine, and in those few seconds, his golden eyes didn't waver in their seriousness or in their directive. Winning both awards was not a goal or an option—it was an order. I had to accomplish it or there'd be serious consequences.

All my life Father had guided me as best he could, and I failed him every single time. He tried to turn me into a colonel; I decided to be a conscientious objector. He asked me to lead a buried treasure expedition; I got them lost. For his birthday party, he asked me to bring wild boars as the festive meal; I brought fruits and vegetables.

He knew I couldn't kill anyone, least of all a scary snake. What did he see in me that I didn't? Perhaps this was a test, and when I failed for the last time, he'd banish me from the Everglades. Where would I go?

I had to get out of the python challenge.

The crowd from the meeting dispersed, crawling, pushing, hissing. Sometimes they'd roll in the water and fight, though not today. They'd have to conserve their energy for slaying pythons. Surely there was another way to remove the exotic snakes.

"Father, do we have to kill?" I asked. "Can't we meditate on it and come up with another plan?"

"You're my successor. How are you going to lead if you can't kill our enemies?" He sounded exasperated and disgusted.

I stepped back.

"Gumbo, we teach by demonstration, not by words." He moved closer, leaning over me. "I want you to kill one python at least sixteen feet long and four or more of any size before sunset tomorrow. Just do it."

What could I say? I nodded. As I pulled back, I nearly knocked Asha over. I zipped around to save her and simultaneously tail-slapped a few gators waiting to speak to Father. They snarled at me but stayed their attack.

"Sorry! Blessings!" I bowed while sidling away. Before I got far, a rock hit my forehead, just missing my left eye. I touched my head—blood. I felt dizzy. I didn't have to search for the culprit.

Cyp and Will darted over.

"Do we have to kill?" Cyp pushed my shoulder.

"Can't we just meditate on it?" Will said with a giggle.

"I'll take care of our tribe while you teach yoga classes."

"Yeah," Will said. "Maybe you'll catch a worm with the help of your big-nosed baby and your dingbat mommy."

I studied Will, hurt that he would insult my friends and me. He quickly hid behind Cyp.

"What others say or do to you has nothing to do with you," Asha said to me, "and everything to do with who they are."

"Clam it!" Cyp said. "Or I'll add mutism to your issues."

I positioned myself on all fours, and Bix clambered onto my back.

"He'll catch a big one!" Bix yelled. "You'll see!"

Asha stepped on, and I immediately raced out of there.

How could I avoid killing a python? No, plural—*pythons.* Four, he'd said, plus one at least sixteen feet long. An option would be to catch them for Father. I could design a snare out of branches and vines. Who was I kidding? I couldn't even wait on the sidelines to trap them.

This was a disaster.

Wait. Perhaps I'd be too busy helping someone in need and wouldn't have time. Yes, that was a plausible excuse, and I'd create positive karma.

I let a few scenarios scuttle through my mind before I settled on human beings. Those biologists driving around on airboats and trucks might need assistance. I listened for the airboat that I'd heard during the meeting. The engine still whined, not too far from us. Curiously, another airboat echoed farther away.

"We're going to find that airboat nearby." I started running.

"Destiny," Asha said.

"Adventure! I'm loving it!" Bix yelled.

Destiny or adventure, anything was better than seeking out pythons. Anything was better than killing. I'd rather die here, today, or tomorrow, if it came to that.

ELEVEN

Runaway

Mr. Dale guided the airboat through channels lined with cypress and other tall trees. Judging by the overgrown plants, I would never have seen this area on a regular tour, so it was kind of cool. Still, this ride might have been a mistake. Instead of eating dinner at a restaurant, I ate my third nut bar.

To my right, a river otter peeked out of the water, a bullhead fish firmly in his mouth. He studied me and my nut bar before slipping back into the water.

"Hey, you guys just missed a river otter," I said.

We searched for him, but he never resurfaced.

"Them otters can get feisty." Mr. Dale puckered his thin lips and continued ahead.

In the next tree island, something massive glimmered among the green. I blinked a couple of times, but it still looked like a ginormous snake coiled at the base of a shrub. No way. It was sci-fi-movie big!

"Is that a python?" I asked.

"Where?" Dad stood up and nearly fell over because Mr. Dale sped up.

A chill spiraled through me at the thought of that jumbo python killing me. First it would hook its razor teeth on my legs, squeeze its muscular body around me, and constrict my blood flow until I suffocated to death. Finally it would swallow me whole, headfirst. How awful.

A bit farther ahead, we slowed through a narrow channel.

"Them yonder are raccoons." Mr. Dale pointed at two odd-looking raccoons on our far left. One had bushy hair just at the top of his head while the other one had shiny, flat hair. I hoped those two raccoons didn't go anywhere near that tree island with the snake; otherwise, they'd be ghosts.

Mr. Dale puttered the airboat along the outer edge of a channel flanked by fifty-foot bald cypress. We faced two possible exits: the first, deep and wide; the second, shallow and narrow.

Ellen frowned at the deeper waterway, dark and crowded with mature trees. I got a bad feeling too, as if something dangerous waited within the shadows.

"I don't think we should go in there," Ellen said.

Mr. Dale's tense expression relaxed.

"It might be the way out," I said, "even though it looks creepy." I accented *creepy* and pitched my voice high.

Mr. Dale gave me the evil eye. "I ain't chicken."

"Ocean is right," Dad said. "That's the direction we should go. It might lead to more open areas while the other one could be a dead end." Dad searched our surroundings and the skies. "And based on where the sun is, this should take us northeast."

Hope at last.

Ellen glanced at Dad, seeming comforted by his words. This late birthday gift should turn out fine.

"It's yer call. Don't go blamin' me if we get lost." Mr. Dale adjusted his hat.

Unreal. Of course it was his fault. I wanted to say something. Then I remembered Sai Baba's quote that Mom would say to me sometimes. *Before you speak, ask yourself: Is it kind, is it necessary, is it true, does it improve on the silence?* Well, it only passed one out of the four. I wouldn't normally remember to go through that list. But since Ellen hadn't said anything, I wouldn't either.

As we cruised through the quiet swamp, strong scents of musty trees layered with lichen and algae drifted past my nose. The area was breathtaking and kind of peaceful.

A pileated woodpecker puffed his body and head, screaming his eerie call from high atop a cypress tree. I cringed as the hairs on my body rose like porcupine quills.

Crackling and crawling noises of nearby insects and spiders made Ellen rub her arms. Wondering what had made the sounds, I searched the closest trees and found several Florida bark scorpions scurrying up a trunk.

Up ahead and above us, a yellow rat snake about sixteen inches long clumsily slithered along a branch, just learning how to climb. I hoped it wouldn't fall on my head if we passed under it.

To our right, dense bushes bounced, as though an animal—a bear?—planned to spring from them, like in the movies.

The shaking stopped, and Mr. Dale sighed.

I made a fart noise with my hand for laughs.

"That ain't me," Mr. Dale said.

Mom patted my thigh to say stop it.

Swimming toward the same shrub, a water snake paused before quickly reversing direction. I glanced at the bushes again.

A deep, guttural snarl rumbled from the throat of a skinny panther wearing a tracking collar. He sounded as if he were ordering us to leave. I think all our mouths dropped to our feet. I'd read panthers didn't normally attack, though they might chase us if we ran. We're supposed to make ourselves appear larger. At the same time, we should give them space so they could escape safely.

Into the stunned silence, Mr. Dale screamed. A bee that had been buzzing around him dug its stinger into his eyelid.

"Argh!" Mr. Dale stomped the gas pedal, and the airboat twirled and zoomed away from the panther.

And then, as I'd feared, the yellow rat snake on the branch—now above me—fell on my head. "Ugh!" I threw it off, and it landed on Mr. Dale's head.

He shrieked louder than the boat's engine.

The airboat zoomed out of the cypress stand, teetering left and right.

A few seconds later, Mr. Dale stepped off the gas. Nothing. The crazy speed continued. My parents and I watched in horror as Mr. Dale pounded the pedal—it appeared to be stuck in fast mode. When he stomped it hard again, the pedal flicked to the left and out of the boat, gone for good. Bye-bye! We were on a runaway airboat!

Mr. Dale tried to peel the snake off his head and neck. The snake curved around, angling for his mouth, then seemed frightened—a normal reaction after seeing Mr. Dale's teeth. Now choking him, the snake clung to Mr. Dale, who struggled until he finally flung it off. With his face wet and his left eyelid ballooning from the bee's sting, he couldn't see very well. Not good.

We were heading straight for a tree island!

"Turn!" my parents yelled, waving their arms like air traffic controllers in case Mr. Dale couldn't hear them. "Turn the boat!"

Mr. Dale finished wiping his one good eye. He yanked the rudder back and cut a quick left. Then he pushed it forward to spin us right to avoid another tree island.

The airboat tilted too far right and hit a bump too fast, and Ellen and I flew off like a trampoline jump, then we screamed right before we smacked into trees.

Everything went dark.

TWELVE

No Thing

 While we moseyed along a mixed marsh near a waterway, the airboat's engine shrilled in the distance as if panicked.

I dipped my head into the water to sense subtle tremors, but finding the precise location of the airboat wasn't easy because it was too far away.

Then shockingly a sudden blast sounded, followed by trees breaking apart and the engine winding down.

"What was that?" Bix asked.

"I'm not sure." Never having seen an accident, I didn't know. But what else could it be? The biologists or other humans might be injured.

Be of service.

I'd go to their aid and they'd keep me busy, too busy to search for pythons.

Another airboat started up, perhaps the second one I'd heard before.

"We should investigate," I said.

"Your father won't be happy even if you're helping someone," Asha said.

She was right, of course. Had she ever been wrong?

"We'll just see if they're okay. That's fine, right?"

"Dear Gumbo, always go with your gut feeling." Asha squeezed my stomach.

I pretended to feel the feathery pinch. "My gut is telling me to investigate."

"Whatever happens was meant to be. Just don't get us killed." She laughed.

"I'm excited to help someone," Bix said. "It'll be my first time."

We pushed through a deeper wet marsh where the slippery ground created perfect conditions for a slide, a fun way to get to the airboat sooner. I raced on my toes, then flopped on my belly, skidding and letting it take me to my destination.

Bix howled with excitement. Asha flapped her wings wildly.

As we decelerated, something whitish shimmered up ahead. I couldn't tell what it was until it was too late. I frantically tried to break my slide.

I crashed into an enormous shed snakeskin, its long strands wrapping around me. The mutant python's scent hovered around my nostrils, overpowering my own. The python might be nearby, slithering, hiding, waiting. If he didn't attack me now, he'd find me someday. It was inevitable. With those thoughts, the snakeskin became a noose around my neck, and I hyperventilated.

Asha and Bix stepped off.

"Gumbo, what's wrong?" Bix asked. He snooped inside one section of the thin, translucent membrane, and his long nose poked through.

I would have laughed if I hadn't been paralyzed.

Just then, about twenty yards away, I saw Cyp and Will gaping at us. They sprinted, fell on their faces, slid, and slammed into me. When Cyp rose on his hind legs, he grabbed the snakeskin.

"What the—" Cyp stretched it out.

Trembling, Will said, "We need to tell Father."

"Of course you didn't catch this python," Cyp said to me. "Look at you." He tossed the snakeskin back.

"You okay, Gumbo?" Will asked, watching me gasp for air. He sounded genuinely concerned, like the good brother he'd been before.

Cyp slapped Will's head. "Let's go. We'll let Gumbo catch this python while we get the rest." He laughed.

Asha ripped the shed snakeskin away and swathed me in her wings.

"My love, one love, all is well. It's nothing. A *no thing*."

I lifted my head to look up at her and said, "Thank you, Asha."

She was an older sister to me; Bix, a baby brother.

Even though I loved them both very much, my heart still longed for Mother.

As youngsters, I spent more time with Mother than anyone. I'd swim just under her while she held me close with one arm. At other times, we'd lounge and bask in a shallow wetland blanketed with duckweed. I especially loved riding on her head, learning about life and laughing at her funny stories. I missed her so much.

After we lost Mother, Will had decided to hang out with Cyp instead of me. I'd become so lonely with no one to share my concerns, my dreams, my hopes. Then I met Asha, then Bix, and my life became joyful again.

I snuggled against Asha's warmth and meditated.

After some time, a helicopter hummed in the distance. I heard sounds that suggested it landed, then took off again.

Feeling more centered, I exhaled and flipped around so Asha and Bix could ride my back.

Everything is for your benefit.

Yes. All were lessons for me to grow spiritually. Someday, with Asha's help, I hoped to be like her: living as a spirit, awake and aware. Someone who didn't let others disturb his peace and joy. Someone who lived without fear and all its negative extensions.

I had to reach enlightenment. Because living like a frightened lizard was no life at all.

THIRTEEN

Everything

Wherever this was, I didn't want to leave. I lay on the soft grass in a wide-open prairie, where bright-colored flowers, trees, and plants glowed. The breeze smelled sweet too. Maybe this was heaven.

Everything pulsed with a steady hum.

"*Ohhh . . . mmm . . .*"

That was it, that *om* sound. I had attended one yoga class with Mom, and everyone chanted that before and after class. Hearing it all around me, I relaxed even more.

Interesting. Above my belly, the sunlight glittered, then the glitter turned into shapes of animals, insects, and trees. The weird part? The light trickled into me, tingling as if it were changing each cell in my body. After it stopped, I felt different, as though I shined like the stars in the universe. Unreal.

Suddenly the grass grew into my skin, and I became the grass. Yet I wasn't scared. The roots—my roots—reached and intertwined through the damp soil, connecting with other roots nearby. I tasted greenness on my lips, like wheatgrass juice. In the next instant, I became a pretty wildflower, and the sunshine warmed my petals.

I loved everything. I was everything. This was heaven for sure.

Then I was a tree, feeling the strength of my solid trunk, my outstretched branches, and my symmetrical leaves. I felt the roots pump water and nutrients to my trunk. Cool.

An instant later I zoomed back into my body. Who was I? How did I get here? As I tried to remember, a deer ambled toward me.

"Wake up!" he said.

And I jolted awake, as though stopping myself from falling off a skyscraper. When I tried to get clearheaded, squinting at the blue sky, the clouds shape-shifted into different animals, and the animals—black rhino, hawksbill turtle, orangutan, and more—scudded across in fast-forward mode before dissipating.

I took the cotton out of my one ear and stuffed it in my pants pocket. The one on the other side must have fallen out.

The sound of a zipper screeched behind me.

Slowly, painfully, with my head pounding, I lifted myself onto my elbows. Ellen lay unconscious a few feet away, breathing normally, no outward signs of injury. Her dog carrier moved, so Nano must be awake.

Sand kicked at my neck and back. Behind me, a river otter hustled away with my waist pack and water canister. No way! I needed those. I scrambled to my feet with surprising speed and tackled the river otter.

His slippery body wriggled as I climbed over him. He smelled of fish, algae, and muck. He swung the pack wildly. I finally snatched it and rolled off.

The otter immediately straddled me. "It's mine now, uggy boy."

"Huh?" He sounded like a squeaky door, yet I clearly understood him as if his gibberish translated immediately into English in my mind.

He grabbed my waist pack, slapped my face, and escaped through the trees.

Before going after him, I checked on Nano and Ellen. Nano poked his head out. Neither of them seemed hurt. I quickly scanned for the airboat and dangerous animals. The area was silent, vast, and empty.

Ellen would be okay for a few minutes.

"Take care of her, Nano. I'll be back."

Nano nodded.

I went to the tree island where the river otter had entered. He was at the far end. I could make out the strands of his fur, his whiskers twitching with excitement, his nubby ears, and the folds of his skin—all as clear and sharp as if he were just inches from me. My vision must be at least three times better than before. Even weirder? I could smell him from where I stood.

Moving across the island without a sound, I crept behind the otter, sitting with my waist pack beside him. He unwrapped a nut bar.

Perfect time. I seized my pack. He twisted around, and using his head, he shoved me back. But I quickly sidestepped. He rammed a tree and toppled. After I made sure he was okay, I laid him gently on a driftwood plank and placed the nut bar in his hand. Finally I sent him off into the waterway so he'd be far from us.

I buckled the pack around my waist with the water canister still full.

The area—waterways interweaving between young mangroves and patches of small tree islands—showed no signs of the airboat or our parents. It wasn't sunny anymore, and the air felt colder.

Hold it. Something was off-kilter.

Everything seemed brighter, glowing with energy like in the dream, only not as intense. The trees swayed and appeared to be watching me. Tiny yellow flowers moved, almost winking their petals. The water glistened like it was alive. Even the sand on my shoes sparkled. This couldn't be real. I had a concussion. That was the only explanation for this mind trip.

But I *had* understood the river otter. Maybe Yaha had given me the gift of understanding animal languages. That would be incredible! Possibly a lifesaver, if it were true.

Before heading back to Ellen, I broke two branches from a tree to use as walking sticks and stripped off the leaves.

Lost and alone without a survival kit, with little food and water, with scary animals roaming around and only two sticks for weapons—I had no clue what we should do next, except find our parents. I rushed back to Ellen, anxious for us to get moving before dark.

I could handle this. Someone had to lead. I could show everyone, especially Ellen, that I was mature and responsible enough to save us all. Ocean River, the hero, instead of the goofy, clumsy kid.

FOURTEEN

Gatorcoccal Madeupitis

The slough caressed my scales and soothed my emotions. I was so grateful to the life-giving and life-sustaining water.

With Asha and Bix on my back, I continued up the waterway bordered by sawgrass, bayhead tree islands, and willow heads. Interestingly, forty feet or more in front of me, a river otter floated on a drifting plank.

An alligator surfaced near him. He used his snout to push the plank along, and my heart faltered. The innocent little otter might become a meal, and I couldn't let that happen.

"A short detour," I said to Asha and Bix.

Once the alligator reached a small tree island, he slipped the otter into his jaw, then clumped toward dense foliage.

I propelled my muscular tail faster to catch up with him and stopped at the island's edge to let Asha and Bix get off.

"Please stay here. I'll be right back." I tracked the alligator on foot.

"I'm a bad boy," the otter murmured to himself as if dreaming. He giggled, possibly tickled by the sharp teeth digging into his armpit. In his hand, he clutched something.

Silently I approached the thicket where the otter had disappeared, and I parted the shrubs, unsure what to do. The alligator, surrounded by his family of twelve juveniles and a wife, rolled the otter out of his mouth. The otter's eyes snapped open.

I'd have to leave right now or do something.

The alligator family stepped closer to the otter, their white teeth dripping saliva.

"Namaste." I moved out from cover and stood upright. "Gumbo, son of the king, here. I just came back from the doctor and wanted to warn you about a disease spreading through the area. I have gatorcoccal madeupitis. Extremely contagious. And the otter has it too." I'd thought of using a fake illness after seeing the red bump on the otter's head.

In unison, the alligators stepped back from us, eyeing each other, not sure whether to believe me. The alligator kids huddled behind their parents and cried, "Afraid. Afraid. Afraid."

The river otter widened his eyes, then frowned at me and tightened his grip on whatever he was holding.

"Look, the first signs are ugly cuts and growths on your body. I have one starting right here." I pointed to the cut on my forehead. "And the otter has it worse. It's on the top of his head, and that unsightly growth is about to burst into a contagious sore."

The otter touched his bump and winced, not realizing it protruded almost an inch.

The alligator family took another step back, and the adults exchanged concerned glances.

Using their moment of hesitation to escape, the otter bolted out toward the slough.

The adult alligators didn't pursue him, and I knew why. The twelve babies across from me were the only survivors out of thirty or more hatchlings.

"No worries," I said. "The bacteria should die off in a few hours, then you'll be safe. All is well."

When I left them, I heard the river otter yelling as he jumped into the water.

"I'm gonna get you for this, uggy boy! I'm gonna find you and make your life a nightmare!"

FIFTEEN

See My Back

As I headed back across the small island, I thought about our situation. I never expected to be lost and alone with Ellen. Trying to survive the wilderness with someone who didn't want to be with me wasn't going to be fun.

Though I thought she'd agree that our first job would be to search for our parents. They'd never leave without us. Unless they got into an accident and died. Then Ellen and I would be orphans. No. I refused to believe that.

When I reached Ellen, two raccoons hovered over her. They were the strange raccoons we'd seen earlier.

Nano hid inside the carrier. Bad doggie.

"Get away from me!" Ellen yelled.

"Hey, shoo!"

They scampered away, just far enough for us to watch them.

"You okay, Ellen?"

"I think so. You?"

"I'm fine, just some bruises."

After I helped her up, I handed her one of my handmade walking sticks.

"Thanks," she said.

I kept my eye on the raccoons for signs of rabies or any sudden moves while I sat down to shake out the sand from my shoes and tuck the bottom of my pants inside my socks to protect against ticks. As Ellen dusted herself, she flung sand on my sneaker tabs before I had the chance to close them. Now the rough side didn't stick as tight to the fuzzy side anymore. They had stretched out too. The 3D printer needed better details and materials. Oh well, at least I had shoes.

"Nano, you okay?" Ellen asked.

He nodded.

Ellen ran from one end of the tree island to the other. "Mom! Mom! Dear God, please let our parents be safe." She rubbed her forehead. "What do you think happened to them?"

Acting like a detective analyzing the situation, I said, "Mr. Dale couldn't stop the airboat, so either they crashed somewhere nearby and we can find them, or they're safe and looking for us. I bet the airboat crashed because it couldn't be stopped."

"I wish my cell phone wasn't broken," Ellen said. "Don't you have yours?"

"Nope. You know my parents. Cell phones, social media, friends, internet, video games, TV, sugar—all under the control of Mama and Papa Bear." Even though Dad had placed EMF protection stuff on my cell phone and earbuds, my parents didn't want me to use it much and definitely not when I was with them.

"I knew we shouldn't have come on this ride unprepared!"

Regular airboat tours had a set route and professional drivers. Mr. Dale didn't have a route, and I bet he was a ticket guy, not a driver. My parents had taken us on this tour even though it was late in the day because they thought Ellen and I would be friends again. Instead, without enough water, we might become jerky treats, or worse, dead much sooner from an animal attack.

"I can handle it. I'll get us out of here," I said.

"You. Really."

It would take time, but she'd trust me again. This was my chance to prove myself.

"We have—"

"—a map."

The raccoons had approached silently and stood a few feet from us.

Ellen stepped beside me, pointing her walking stick at them.

"I'm Peeka," said the strange-haired raccoon.

"And I'm Boo." His voice was silky smooth, just like his hair.

"How can I understand them?" Ellen stammered. "Did you hear them say they're Peeka and Boo?"

I spoke like a TV announcer. "We've entered another dimension filled with smelly animals and a ghost." My throat felt dry and ticklish, so I sipped water from my canister.

"What are you saying?"

"The ghost—Yaha—he gave us the gift to talk with animals so they can help us. This means we're definitely lost and alone because that's the only time he does that, remember?"

"Ghost, he"—Nano moved his paw above his head— "like that to you." He pointed to us both.

"Nano! Baby, I can understand you!" Ellen hugged him and kissed his cute forehead. "This is so incredible! I have so many questions for you, but first what else did the ghost do?"

"Sad face. Flew away."

"If you see him again, can you let us know? Maybe he can help us."

Nano nodded, then barked, "Bathroom!"

Ellen set him down to do his business.

"I think Yaha gave us other gifts too," I said. "Don't you feel different? I feel more energy. My hearing and eyesight are sharper. I can even smell more stuff." I rubbed my nose. "Though I wish I couldn't."

I studied the raccoons. I'd kicked them out of bird feeders at home without noticing a scent. Maybe Yaha had given us more of those olfactory receptors Dad talked about.

Ellen always smelled sweet and clean. Now another scent drew me to her.

"I don't know," she said, glancing around. "I feel fine considering we had an accident, so yeah, maybe I do feel different. You know, things do seem brighter and more intense or something."

I faced the raccoons. "I'm Ocean, she's Ellen, and the pup is Nano."

Peeka and Boo seemed friendly.

"So you have a map?" I asked.

Peeka lifted the weird bushy hair—which was actually a toupee—and pulled out a folded dried leaf and handed it to me. Gross. I really didn't want to touch the map. I held a small corner and flapped it around, airing it out for a few seconds.

Crudely drawn on a dried palm leaf, the map had no directions, only a few marks and notes: *hot babe, fun babe,* and *nice babe.* Great. A useless map from playboy raccoons.

"I'll be sure to use this map if I want to date a raccoon. Like never!"

Peeka pointed to a spot on the map.

"This is where—"

"—we are now," Boo said.

Peeka touched one *X* mark. "These areas are—"

"—where we have seen humans." Boo touched the other *X.*

I frowned. "Dudes, what happened to your hair?"

Peeka narrowed his eyes at Boo, who ignored him.

"Peeka's ex-girlfriend scalped him!" Boo giggled.

"Boo's girlfriend gave him a keratin treatment!" Peeka stroked Boo's hair.

Boo slapped his hand away and tipped Peeka's toupee off-center.

I thought I was strange, but they beat me ten times over. I liked them!

"You're the same raccoons we saw earlier?" I asked.

They nodded and pushed closer.

"We would like a—"

"—barter. An exchange."

"You want some yummy-tummy snack?" I unwrapped one bar, split it in two, and gave them the pieces. "Boy, the nut bars are a hit." Mom sold all kinds of variations on her website, but I'd suggest she expand into the pet food market. Our pets would love them for sure. "I especially love the nuts."

Ellen rolled her eyes. "Yeah, that makes sense."

If we were still besties, that would have been funny, but now it sounded like sarcasm.

The raccoons sniffed. They nibbled. "Delicious," Boo said.

"So you guys can draw and write maps?" Ellen seemed skeptical.

"We study—"

"—at special schools."

"But can't—"

"—pronounce human words."

"I guess animals have schools too," Ellen said. "Did you guys see an airboat around here?"

"We didn't see—"

"—a thing."

"We're looking—"

"—for a friend."

They glanced at each other.

"Well, thanks for the map!" Then I said to Ellen, "I think the airboat went that way after we fell off, and the two areas Peeka and Boo marked, where tourists might hang out, are in that same direction." We might run into people even if the boat wasn't there.

"Hold on. Shouldn't we stay here in case our parents come looking for us? Build a tent or something? It's going to be dark soon."

"Nah, boo that idea," I said.

Boo stared at me, scratching his head.

"You don't even know where the airboat went," Ellen said. "You're just guessing."

I squared my shoulders and acted like a military officer. "Ma'am, please follow orders. I've got the map. I also have an internal GPS, my mapdar. *Beep, beep, beep.*" I placed one hand on my head and moved it around as if it were receiving GPS signals.

"Are you getting a signal that you're acting like a five-year-old?"

I pointed the mapdar at her, and in a fast beat, I said, "*Beep, beep, beep, beep, beep.* The signal says, 'Kiss my heinie.'"

Yeah, it was childish, but we needed some lightness. Things didn't look good for us.

"Wait," Ellen said. "Let's think about this."

"See me, see my back." There was no time to waste. I spun around and left.

She'd follow me. I was sure of it.

"Stop! Ocean! We'll be in worse trouble if we get separated."

"I have to find them. There are gators, panthers, and pythons in the swamp!"

"Let's focus for a moment." Ellen sprinted after me.

I sped ahead. *Focus*—her favorite word. To her, *focus* meant we'd spend hours analyzing the situation and make a list of options. Before we knew it, it'd be dark and we, or our parents, would be dead.

"Stop!"

I waded through ankle-deep water among young mangroves. Deeper waterways might hold alligators. Well, at least it wasn't summertime. Ellen and I would be swimming just to get from one part of the land to the next, not to mention fighting swarms of mosquitoes. It'd be horrible.

Now at least fifty or more paces ahead of Ellen, I stopped to review the map and wait for her to catch up. A few yards in front of me, two small tree islands bunked next to each other, just as the map showed. Peeka and Boo said this spot had humans, but I didn't see anyone camping or any signs that people even came around.

"Ugh!" Half-inch-long red ants bit my face, hands, and stomach. I slapped them off and jumped up and down, trying to stomp them while moving away from several ant mounds.

Ellen muttered, "I wish I were stuck with someone more mature."

"What did you say?" At forty feet away, I still heard her. I could even hear her breathing.

She stopped walking and blinked a few times. "I said, stop being so immature."

I winced—the same words from the funeral. Was she ever going to forgive me?

She hurried toward me. "We have to focus," she said in a calmer voice. "We're in serious trouble, and it'll be dark soon. We can't wander around getting more lost and—dancing!"

Nano frowned from the carrier.

"I wasn't dancing! Fire ants were biting me!"

"Well, sorry. That's not what it looked like."

With the bites hurting, the stress of being in an accident, and the possibility our parents were hurt or dead, I wanted to scream and cry.

"I know you want to wait in case they come looking for us. But what if they're unconscious somewhere? What then, Ellen? What will gators or pythons do when they find them at night? Can you honestly stay here while it's still daylight and just hope they'll show up? I won't. I'll do whatever it takes to find my parents even if I die trying."

Her eyes became red and watery.

"FYI, I'm very mature for my age because of my parents. Everyone has told me that. Sure, yeah, I screwed up at the funeral. It wasn't on purpose. I was thinking about your dad and how he wanted us to always smile, and I just—" I gulped down air and fought back the tears. "I'll get us out of here as I promised, and you know what? Maybe I'll dance goofy or clown around to lighten the mood. At least I won't be unfun like you."

I took off faster than before.

This was all too much. These past few months had been emotional and draining, and now it was more of the same junk. I wasn't sure how much cleansing I needed, but I was done with it.

Then I felt bad. Ellen had it worse than me, and I'd never been mad at her before. I slowed down to hear and smell her behind me. She kept sniffling. Why did it hurt to see her in pain? I guess because I still loved her as my best friend even if, technically, we weren't friends anymore.

When I first met her at the Conservancy for one of their summer day camps, I thought Ellen—with her kind, gentle brown eyes—was the prettiest girl in the whole world. I could tell she loved animals and nature as much as I did, so I introduced myself.

It took her a few seconds to say hello because she was adorably shy.

Once I put on my funny sunglasses with the springing eyeballs, Ellen giggled. Right away I knew we'd be close friends.

Now I was sorry, but not for leaving to search for our parents. I knew that people should stay put in situations like this, and if our parents were with us, then sure, we should remain where we were. This was different. Our parents could be hurt and defenseless. I kept thinking about that jumbo python and all those gators, and that made me scared.

But I needed to be brave, just like the song Ellen was singing to her dad right now.

SIXTEEN

Grand Mission

 As I glided through the slough with Asha and Bix on my back, I noticed a young girl near pockets of small tree islands.

"Oh look, a human girl," Bix said.

It had taken me some effort to put aside Father's python challenge. I reminded myself I was meant for a different purpose today, that it would be revealed to me, and that all I had to do was send out positive intentions. The answer was clear: rescuing her must be the grand mission.

I swam faster, sweeping my tail. When I reached the bank, Asha and Bix slid off, and I rose from the water. The girl shrieked and fell on her backside. I shouldn't have stood upright, scaring her.

Within seconds, a young boy appeared and blocked her from me, a stick held out in front of him. How had he moved so quickly? I hadn't seen him. He stared at me as if he were a hawk ready to attack. He was so brave!

"Are you okay?" the boy asked the girl.

I understood him clearly, as if he spoke our language. Even though my royal family studied level-one reading and writing English, Spanish, and Muscogee, we couldn't vocalize the words and couldn't retain anything complex. But through my intuition and the vibrational sound waves, I always comprehended what humans said, or at least I thought I did. This time there was no doubt.

"I'm okay," the girl replied.

Judging by the fierce way the boy protected the girl, they were good friends. Both of them might be a year or two younger than me. I was fourteen in alligator years, not sure what the equivalent was in human years.

Bix waddled from the water and gave them a warm smile. Asha posed near a tree, facing away from us, possibly communicating with spirits. She could see and telepathically converse with them. I couldn't, and I was grateful.

"Namaste. I'm Gumbo, this is Bix, and she is Asha. We're here to serve you in any way we can. Today, tomorrow, however long you need us. We're flexible." I spread my arms and ended with a bow and my hands clasped in prayer.

Bix tapped my foot. "What about the promise to your dad?"

I did a yoga forward bend to pick him up, then I placed him on my shoulder. "Helping others is more important even if it means I'll be too busy to keep that promise." I closed my eyes, crossing my fingers for added measure.

"Stay back, Ellen. Gators are deadly no matter what they say."

"Gumbo? Deadly?" Bix chuckled. "He's not like other gators. He doesn't eat anything with eyeballs. We're nice animals." Bix hugged my head.

When the girl named Ellen moved next to the boy, a puppy peeked from a pouch on her outfit. He and Bix exchanged a friendly wave. They might be around the same age.

"You seem to be that," Ellen said.

Asha expanded her wings to our surroundings. "We are all *that*."

The humans covered their ears at the immense sound of Asha's voice while the dog disappeared into the girl's pouch.

Mourning doves lifted into the air, whistling as they screamed, "Danger! Danger!" They defecated on the boy's hair, shirt, and shoes.

"Wait! Don't go!" Ellen yelled. "They could have helped us." She sighed and patted her dog.

"Call me the poop magnet," the boy said. He casually searched the ground for leaves to scrape off what he could from his hair and clothing.

"Nice! Keep doing your art! Love you!" Bix waved to the doves and studied the streaks of bird excrement on the boy's shirt, nodding appreciatively. "Much better than the plain blue."

"Jackson Pollock's finest," the boy said.

Ellen glanced at the boy, then quickly turned, trying not to laugh. Her little dog giggled. I didn't get the joke.

"I'm Ocean," the boy said, "and this is Ellen and Nano."

Ellen stepped forward. "Don't you think it's odd we can talk to you?"

"Yaha," Asha replied. She stared intently at Ellen.

So the legend was true. He was one of the spirits Asha spoke to regularly.

"I think I saw you with hundreds of alligators," Ocean said.

"Yes." I assumed he meant the recent meeting. "Was it your airboat that passed us?"

"Yep. I saw four gators standing upright, like you are now, instead of being down on all fours. Are you special or something?" He frowned. "You're tall, you can stand for a long time, you have wider shoulders than a regular gator, and you eat only plants?"

"He's of ancient royal blood," Bix replied, pointing to the sky.

Ocean and Ellen both glanced up.

This wasn't the time to discuss my family's history, so I kept quiet.

"Each of us is unique," Asha shouted to a fly buzzing around her. "With a divine purpose." The fly zipped away.

Ocean moved closer to Asha. "Are you some kind of guru?"

"No, I'm a silly old bird. The guru is within." She laughed.

Ocean took a few steps back and rubbed his ears.

"We heard the engine, followed by a loud bang," I said.

"We're not sure if it crashed or if the sound was something else. That's why we're here to investigate and help."

"Ellen, did you hear that?"

"No," Ellen smirked.

Ocean smiled and said to me, "We fell off the airboat, and our parents were still on it. And even though I don't want to believe it, I bet it was their airboat that crashed. Could you take us to where you heard the bang?"

"I thought it was right here. Sorry."

Ellen stepped closer to me. "Do you know where people hang out or where there's a tour?"

"I'm not aware of such places, and I've only seen biologists and a few people drive around in an airboat or truck." I wondered if I could assist them after all. Birds could certainly help if they came near us.

Ocean faced Asha and hollered, "Can you fly! And tell us! Where to go! Or if there are humans nearby?" He smiled.

"Wing challenged, visually challenged, and aurally challenged," I answered for Asha.

"You forgot follicly challenged," Ocean said, smiling at Asha's bald head.

"We are all challenged to remember who we are," Asha said to a hummingbird, who quickly disappeared behind a fire bush.

Just then, the sounds of an airboat reverberated in the distance. It might have been the same airboat that had been stopping and starting up for the past hour or so.

"Do you hear that?" Ocean sounded excited.

Ellen shook her head at Ocean and said to me. "We accept your offer of help."

"Let's go find that airboat." Ocean took off without waiting for us.

Bix said, "Adventures with our new friends!"

Nano frowned.

"Sorry, Gumbo," Ellen said. "We have to follow him. We can't be separated."

We scooted behind Ocean, the leader. I sensed that he might be another teacher. What had Asha always said? A teacher appeared when the student was ready. Or was it the student who appeared when the teacher was ready?

As we tramped through ankle-deep water, we avoided the depths where our new friends couldn't pass. After a brief hike, we came upon a six-foot sawgrass wall.

When Ocean tried to push the sedge away, he cut his hand on its serrated edges, so he slapped the sawgrass with his stick.

"Never do harm." Asha leaned her face close to Ocean's, her right eye flickering while she spoke. "There is always another way." She swung her walking stick, and we all ducked, Ocean and Ellen barely in time. Using her stick, she bent the sawgrass at the bottom, creating a walkway to prevent contact with the sedge.

"Cool," Ocean said. Then he yelled, "Kiyap!" and led the way as if he were performing martial arts. Bix clapped, enjoying Ocean's performance.

Ellen frowned, yet she followed his leadership, so she must trust him.

After getting through the sawgrass, we arrived at a mixed marsh, and by now the airboat only whispered in the skies.

Ocean reviewed a set of sketches on what appeared to be a dried palm leaf, and Ellen sipped water from her container.

"Are you sure this is the right way?" Ellen asked Ocean. "I don't hear the airboat anymore." Then she gave me a pleading look.

With no intention of taking the lead, I started chanting mentally, using my mala beads.

"Who's got the map? Oh yeah, me." Ocean flailed the leaf at her.

I stopped chanting. Ocean and Ellen stood motionless as well. The air had gone quiet, not a murmur from insects or animals and no breeze, as though the wind held its breath. I inhaled deeply. A faint odor scraped past my nostrils, an odor that scared me. Could it be my imagination?

I asked Ocean, "May I see the map, please?"

He handed it over, watching my trembling hands, which only made me more self-conscious. I was certain he'd never met a coward like me.

The markings on the map didn't make sense. I couldn't tell which way was north or south, so I searched for familiar landmarks. Here was the sawgrass wall we'd just gone through—

Ocean snatched the map from my hands and set off again. "It's straight ahead."

Straight ahead, there could be danger. I chanted faster, not sure which direction we should go. Back through the sawgrass? I hastened behind Ocean.

An eastern cottontail rabbit zoomed past us, frightened and panting, not stopping or looking back. My heart rate accelerated.

After a few seconds, Ocean halted so abruptly that Ellen bumped into him.

Then I smelled it. Right before I heard it.

"I think you'll pair nicely with a bottle of 1953 Petrus."

SEVENTEEN
Biggie Mouth

Twenty feet away, a jumbo Burmese python stared at us. We all turned our heads to look behind us, hoping he was speaking to someone else. The area was dead silent.

He was probably the one I'd seen earlier under the shrub. The length of his body stretched out about thirty feet, and he was slender—meaning he'd fasted, preparing for a big meal with wine, apparently. He reminded me of an anaconda. His massive head and the width of his body meant he could swallow Ellen and me together.

I froze as that visual entered my mind—inside a python, dissolving in its juices, a lumpy carcass in its body. The others gawked from either side of me. Gumbo trembled so much that the ground around us shook.

"Pardon me, was I drooling?" Behind a leaf, the python wiped his face.

"Just a little," Bix said.

"Better?" The python bared gigantic curved teeth, perfect for hooking his prey.

"You got a biggie mouth like Gumbo!" Bix patted Gumbo's head.

When the python started to hiss, Asha said, "Time to go."

Even though she spoke the words calmly, her voice grated like a hundred birds screaming in my ear—but it did loosen my feet.

I lifted my stiff legs and ran with my arms extended in front, reaching for what, I didn't know. Everyone else ran next to me.

We tore through a wet prairie with scattered trees, scattered sawgrass, and scattered brains. Asha drifted in another direction, and Gumbo grabbed her to keep her close. His tail swung like a music conductor's baton.

"Ahhh!" The python had snagged the end of my shirt! I pushed my stick behind me and stabbed him near his eye. My shirt tore. He flew off, twirled around, and landed with a thud. I fell forward into a shrub, jumped to my feet, and—

The python launched toward my legs and missed because I leaped away like a deer—really, like a deer. And he slammed his face into the mud. How had I jumped that high and far? My legs and body felt springy, strong yet light. Unreal.

The map lay on the ground twenty feet away. As scared as I was, I had to get it back. I couldn't give Ellen more items to add to her "Irresponsible Ocean" list.

With everyone far ahead, I circled to the right, and the python pursued me. He vaulted toward me again, and I jumped away. Even though I was unusually agile and fast, the python trailed right behind me. Every time he got closer, I pushed myself with a force I didn't know I had. Though I'd have to think smart if I wanted to live.

Just then he snapped toward me, and I shot away. He ended up in a shrub, flipped right back out, and sprang two feet into the air, targeting my legs.

Like a blue jay flying up from the ground, I hopped ten feet to a nearby branch. The python thumped his head on the tree trunk and jerked his neck back, confused by my miraculous abilities. Believe me, I was confused too. I didn't have time to think about what I was so effortlessly doing. I jumped down on the other side of the tree, and he slid behind me. I circled the tree, and he was right there. I kept going around the tree with incredible speed, and the python followed until he had wrapped himself around it at least three times.

"*Au revoir*, Biggie Mouth." I waved.

His eyes narrowed when he understood my words, then he fired toward me.

Because of my loose sneakers, I tripped facedown and closed my eyes, feeling the python's energy heading toward me. This was the end. This was how my short life would end: in the belly of a jumbo python.

"Tastes like bird droppings," the python said, spitting.

His mouth had only grazed my long bangs. *Phew!*

"That's okay. The rest of you should be *délicieux*." He scrunched back and tried again to bite me. Nope. Like a rubber band that reached only so far, he snapped back. He began to unfurl from the tree, swinging wildly in reverse. I rose, sprinted, and scooped up the map.

Gumbo must have come back for me. He stood frozen in place; his eyes fastened on the python as if hypnotized. Bix tried to break the spell, jumping and waving on his shoulder.

"Wake up!" I slapped Gumbo's arm.

He started awake and tottered, then fell on me. As I stopped my face from smashing into the mud, my hands dug deep, and the map got buried.

"Ocean, Ocean," Gumbo spluttered as the python squiggled toward us.

"Guys!" Ellen yelled. "He's right behind you!"

She'd come back for me too. Interesting.

"Reckless!" Nano shouted.

I plunged my hands through the mud, searching for the map. Bits of it were all I could find, nothing worth salvaging. Gumbo pulled me up, and I bore down hard on my loose sneakers, pushing away from the ground. We left a moment before the python landed on our spot.

We raced as fast as we could, but the python kept pace as though he had legs. He definitely wasn't a regular python. No snake could move like that. And no matter how fast we ran, he got closer. If we stumbled and fell, we'd be ghosts for sure.

After a few minutes, I didn't hear him behind us anymore. He must have steered in another direction.

Maybe he knew a different way to cut through the forest. If we veered left or right, he might be waiting for us, so we stayed straight.

I had a bad feeling he never failed at getting his meal. I also had a bad feeling we'd see him again.

About ten minutes later, my right sneaker flew off my foot and landed in front of another section of the tree island.

We paused in front of that area so I could put my sneaker back on.

I spoke to Ellen. "I think we lost the python, don't you?"

"No," she replied.

"Me neither," I said, glancing at our only option in front of us, a dark wooded area riddled with cobwebs.

Gumbo played with his beads while his teeth chattered. Well, he was young, maybe close to my age, so I guess he could be afraid of stuff.

Nano's eyes popped, and he dropped into his carrier and cried, "Ghosts!"

"Ghosts or not, we have to go through there." Just as I finished speaking, tormented moans rose from inside the spooky forest. Not good.

EIGHTEEN

Creeper

Creepy moans. Pitch-black shadows. Critters' haven. It wouldn't be my choice to enter a place with all those factors. These dense hammock forests could also be a fortress of trees, making it difficult to find an exit.

I set Asha down, then headed to a St. John's wort plant and consumed a heaping portion of its sweet yet bitter leaves to soothe my nerves.

"What does the map say?" Ellen asked. She frowned at Ocean's empty, muddy hands. "Great, you lost the map. You know what? It doesn't matter because you took us farther away from that airboat. We're more lost than ever."

"I don't see you leading the way. Or knowing the way," Ocean said.

"I don't know the way and neither do you. That's why we should let Gumbo lead."

She had faith in me, though she shouldn't. I continued chewing, my teeth likely green and leafy.

"You didn't have to come along." Ocean scowled.

"Don't blame this on me." Ellen crossed her arms. Then she placed her right hand on her head as in a martial arts knifehand strike and moved it side to side. "Gumbo, he calls this his mapdar. *Beep. Beep. Beep.*"

"Focus. Focus." Ocean jutted his chin out, made a bizarre frowning expression, and danced stiffly.

"That's real mature," Ellen said. She did the mapdar hand again and kicked her legs out while she lunged in a circle.

Bix giggled and clapped. "Love the funny dancing."

"*Whirr, whirr,* error, error," Ellen said.

If they continued fighting, I'd have to excuse myself, my nerves unable to handle constant tension and strife.

"Be serious, life is so serious," Ocean said, still moving without bending arms or legs.

I shoveled more St. John's wort into my mouth and gagged on the excess.

Asha pounded the ground with her walking stick. "There are no errors, only lessons."

Frightened by her loud voice, common grackles squawked rapidly in the distance and darted over the trees.

Ocean and Ellen stopped quarreling, and I was grateful for it. I didn't understand their disagreement because they seemed to be friends.

"Aw, do it again," Bix said.

They kept quiet for a few seconds.

"Sorry. Truce?" Ocean asked Ellen.

Ellen bit her lip. "Yeah, sorry."

Nano said a firm, "Yes."

"Okay, let's go," Ocean said. "*Beep, beep,* this way!"

Ellen glanced at me just as I burped.

"Excuse me," I said.

Once we entered the hammock tree island, my thoughts turned to the cobwebs littering the dense forest. I smelled something surprising, something like the scent of the river otter I'd saved earlier.

"Ghosts!" Nano shrieked. We all jumped, except Asha, then we huddled together before fleeing like scared mice. I grabbed Asha, who was strolling as if she were enjoying a sunny day on the beach.

Less than a minute later, Ellen almost lost her balance and pushed Ocean straight into a spiderweb spanning two trees. Where was the giant spider?

"Help!" Ocean yelled and flounced toward Ellen and me, the silky strands wrapped around his face and body. My heart sped up as Ocean kept coming toward us while we kept flitting away.

"Spider dance." Bix tried to imitate Ocean.

Still thrashing about, Ocean crashed into Asha, who rose to her feet and helped him pluck off the silvery threads.

On the ground, a long vine stretched from one side to the other. Ellen might have tripped over it. Next clue: the scent of the river otter lingered nearby. Could he have been involved? I pivoted to stare at Ocean. Was he the otter's "uggy boy," and did *uggy* stand for *ugly?* Ocean had a pleasing appearance, just like Ellen, so *uggy* couldn't be him.

"Sorry, Ocean. I tripped. You okay?" Ellen sounded sincere.

"Yes," he said in a falsetto voice. He leaned on his walking stick, took in a long breath to steady himself, then said, "I know. You did that on purpose because of the plastic spider prank I played on you a year ago. You promised you'd get back at me."

"No, I didn't. I—Ah!" Suddenly she straddled me, squishing Nano against my chest.

Asha remained calm, as usual, staring into space or, most likely, conversing mentally with ghosts roaming around.

Then I saw what had sent Ellen jumping to my chest— the spiny legs and body of a huge golden silk orb weaver marching on top of Ocean's head.

"Hi, spider! You're my size!" Bix waved.

Ellen pressed harder against me.

"What! Get it off!" Ocean hopped in front of Asha, wriggling like a worm and shaking his head.

Asha's left wing jerked up, flicking the spider off. She kept swinging and slapping Ocean's head. Because of her injury, she sometimes couldn't stop her spasms.

A muffled cry came from Nano, and Ellen released me so the little one could breathe.

"Sorry, baby," Ellen said, petting his head. "Sorry, Gumbo."

Ocean spat feathers before he touched his head and face. "It didn't bite." He half smiled, looking immensely relieved.

"Think positive," I said while frantically searching the ground for the spider. "It's a golden silk orb weaver, also called a banana spider. It normally can't kill you, unless you're allergic to its venom. Then it could be a problem."

"Not venomous but still a creeper." Ellen rubbed her arms. "I don't like spiders, snakes, and roaches."

"Me either," I said.

"You're lucky it wasn't deadly." Ocean frowned at her.

"I'm really sorry. I didn't push you on purpose. You know me. I wouldn't do that to you."

"Uh-huh," Ocean said. "Okay, you're not the lying type." His eyes twinkled. "You're the pain-in-the-butt type." He laughed.

Ellen smiled for the first time since I'd met her.

Ocean caught his breath. He peeled off more webbing while sneaking glances at Ellen.

With everyone calm, I was about to advise them that we should leave, but I felt something feathery crawl up my arm. "The spider!"

Ellen hid behind Ocean.

Asha passed by and swung her good arm. The spider shot through the air and over the trees, pouting all the way. I prayed for his safety.

Bix waved goodbye. "Sorry, spider! Love you!"

Nano waved as well. His was like a get-out-of-here motion. Then his eyes widened, and his straggly hair and body trembled.

Ghostly wails rose from all directions.

A random branch flew over our heads.

Something fluffy scurried past our feet, too fast for us to see.

All of us screamed, except Asha and Bix. As we bolted away from the haunted tree island, Ellen held the back of Ocean's shirt, and I carried Asha and Bix, crouching down, making myself a smaller target for spiders and angry ghosts.

After a few minutes of running, I said, "This way." I led them to an open trail lined with shrubs toward a light at the end of the path.

It looked like a solid choice until a wild boar rammed through a bush, grunting, "Get out!"

"Sorry! Blessings!" I said. As we reversed directions, I heard the boar cooing to her babies.

It was a strange thought given the moment, but I wondered when I would have my own children. Who'd want a cowardly alligator? No one. The thought depressed me. I was a failure as an alligator, as a son, and as a male.

Be gentle with yourself.

Asha had advised me to be the love of my life and to be my best friend. Perhaps she knew I'd be alone without a mate.

Up ahead, about a hundred yards, the glinting light distracted me. We'd reached the end of the ghostly passage, and I inhaled with gratitude.

Before dark, we'd have to build a shelter for Ocean and Ellen. The pineland was the best and safest place; it was dry, and it had plenty of palm fronds for making a tent.

Safety, of course, was an illusion in the Everglades. Every ecosystem had its insects, its plants, its mammals, its reptiles, each with its own deadly players, and the pinelands were no different.

NINETEEN

Nighttime

"Om . . ." Gumbo spread his arms out to the pine trees and saw palmettos. "I feel good energy here. It's the perfect place to sleep."

Twisting sideways in a yoga pose, he let Bix down from his shoulder and sighed. "My chakras are so off-balance."

He bent his right leg and placed the sole of his foot under his left inner thigh: the tree pose. I remembered that from my one yoga class with Mom. He pressed his hands together by his chest and closed his eyes.

We were in a freakish world, for sure, where animals did yoga and chanted with beads, where ghosts and jumbo pythons roamed, where raccoons had strange hairstyles.

Ellen and I exchanged glances. She looked wiped out and a bit dazed. I wondered if she was as close to breaking into tears—or hysterical laughter—as I was.

"We have to keep going," I said. "We need to find our parents." No way were we stopping to do yoga.

Ellen rushed to my side. "Yeah, we can't stop now."

Good. She agreed with me. If we'd stayed where we were before, I bet that python would have found us, and then what? I was also glad we were with Gumbo. I felt safer with someone who knew the land and the dangers.

Gumbo wobbled out of the tree pose. "Dusk, dawn, and nighttime, when animal hunters come out, are the most dangerous times in the swamp. We need time to create a calming, protective space of"—Gumbo spread his arms again—"peace and harmony for you to rest and reenergize for tomorrow."

Ellen frowned. "I'm afraid our parents might be out there."

"And injured," I added. "A gator or panther or that jumbo python might attack them." I shuddered at the thought.

"Trust dissolves all your made-up worries." Asha stepped into a ditch, came out on top of an armadillo, and stepped off as if the move had been planned. The armadillo bustled away.

"Asha always tells me to visualize and say out loud what I want to happen," Gumbo said, "and not what I don't."

"I'm visualizing our parents finding us." I imagined hugging Mom and Dad. "I'm also seeing us eat a thick veggie burger with sweet potato fries and drinking gallons of clean water." I imagined the smell, the feel in my hands, and the taste.

"I want our parents to be safe." Ellen looked teary.

Nano said to Ellen, "Be brave, princess."

That was weird. Mr. Hansen had called her princess

too. I squinted at Nano, and he smiled wide, just like Mr. Hansen.

Asha peered inside a saw palmetto shrub and yelled, "The past is gone. The future isn't here."

The shrub rustled as something scampered away and said, "Thank you."

I'd bet Asha woke up all the animals in the Everglades.

"Aren't you both drained of energy?" Gumbo asked.

"I am a bit tired," I said. Sleeping sounded so good right now. My muscles felt dull and achy like I'd played tennis all day long. Still, I could search for maybe another hour.

"We have to hurry if we want to build a tent." Gumbo fiddled with his beads. His bracelet and necklace were like the ones I'd seen women and men wearing at Mom's yoga studio.

"All right," Ellen said. "I guess we can get an early start in the morning."

Something pricked my hand, and I looked down. A mosquito, her belly filled after biting me, buzzed, "Hello. Thank you." It made me wonder if mosquitoes and gnats who'd whizzed around my ear in the past were just trying to chat with me.

Ellen and I rubbed ourselves with bug wipes and sipped our water. At that point, my canister was less than half full even after I'd taken only small sips. Our water wouldn't be enough if it took us all day tomorrow to get help or find our parents. Right now I wanted to drink the whole thing straight away. I hooked the canister back to my belt.

Bix eyed my waist pack. "I like your purse."

"It's not a purse," I responded quickly. "It's like a mini backpack." Then in the deepest voice I could muster, I added, "We should start to make the tent."

"First clear your mind of all chatter," Asha said. Many insects skedaddled just from her voice, so that was good. "Then connect with your *prana,* your breath, until you feel calm."

After spending a few minutes breathing evenly and erasing all thoughts, Asha taught us the warrior I, II, and III yoga poses to build strength and concentration. Then we used a variation of warrior II pose to sweep the ground using our walking sticks.

I felt fluid and energetic yet peaceful as debris flew neatly to the side. Ellen and I moved in sync, our motions looking like martial arts—one, two, three, and one, two, three, and one, two, three. This was kinda fun. We made a good team, just as we had in the past, playing sports, raising funds for foundations, planting trees, and helping animals.

Nano and Bix played with a pine cone. Well, it was mostly Bix chasing the cone and Nano kicking it away before Bix could bite it. Bix moved fast for a baby turtle.

Asha returned with saw palmetto fronds, and Gumbo brought branches to build a triangular tent between two trees. They showed us how to tie the leaves together for the roof, and we laid a thick layer of the leaves for the bed. Then for the final touch, Gumbo threw plants and herbs inside and around the tent.

We asked Asha to tell us more about Yaha. She only said, "When the time is right, you will know."

"Can you thank him for us?" I asked.

Asha glanced at a saw palmetto nearby. "He already knows you're grateful."

"Doesn't he know the way?" Ellen stared at the same shrub. "You know, to help us find people?"

"If he knew the way back to your tour, he wouldn't have bothered giving you his abilities." Asha laughed. "He's stuck roaming the area where he lost her."

The rest of the bugs around us disappeared. Her voice was a natural insect repellent.

"He's trapped in this earthly plane for an unresolved issue while still in a formless dimension," Gumbo said. "He's there but thinks he's here."

"Just like us," Asha said.

"*Wooo,*" I said, wailing like a ghost. "*Wooo.*"

"Please continue, Gumbo." Ellen waved her hand, telling me to stop.

"He'll continue searching for his love until he lets go of the guilt of losing her. His guilt is keeping him stuck." Gumbo faced Asha.

"Right," Asha said.

"Couldn't you help him know the truth?" Ellen asked.

Asha shrugged. "He won't believe me."

We couldn't pull any new information from them. I'd have to do more research on Eleanor, his love, and Yaha's shape-shifting powers too. Even though I had some heightened physical talents, there was no way I could shape-shift. Maybe such abilities developed later, or maybe we didn't get all his goodies.

Still, it was cool to have zero communication problems with animals even without shape-shifting. With my pets at home, I could guess what they wanted, but I never truly understood them. Too bad we'd lose these powers after we got saved.

By the time our palmetto tent stood ready, the sunset sky had splashed orange, purple, and blue. More than a hundred yards away, a row of six screech owls perching on a pine tree gazed at it too, while a few others scanned the ground, probably for rats and who knew what else.

Maybe half an hour later, inside our makeshift shelter, Ellen and I sat so close I sensed the heat from her body, saw her breath spill into the air, and felt disoriented from her scent.

Gumbo and Asha meditated outside the tent. I had tried meditation with Mom, but I'd only fidget the whole time or fall asleep.

At the tent's edge, Bix and Nano stared at the sky bedazzled with stars.

The bright full moon gave a milky sheen to everything, including the curve of Ellen's forehead, the slope of her nose, and the shape of her lips.

She caught me looking at her. I quickly turned away, glad she couldn't see me blushing.

After a couple of minutes, I peeked at her again, but this time I found her watching me. She bent her head and retied her ponytail.

Interesting. Maybe she was coming around and wanted to be friends again.

After Gumbo and Asha finished their meditation, Bix and Nano stepped into the tent. Nano jumped onto Ellen's lap and twirled around a few times, searching for a comfortable position. Once settled, he sneezed.

"Stinker!" He stared at me.

Just then the stench of intense methane and skunk-like body odor wafted into our enclosed space. Skunk apes were in that legends book. Those creatures didn't exist. Well, I hoped not.

"Skunk ape?" I asked.

"No, your armpit," Ellen replied, biting her lips, eyes sparkling against the moonlight. That wasn't sarcasm but a friendly tease, so it was a good sign.

I exaggerated sniffing my armpit. "Ah, sweatalicious. Maybe you're inhaling my pheromones. I read an article on that." I couldn't tell if it was me, but it stank in there for sure.

"It's called B.O. They have stuff for that, you know." She smiled.

Bix inhaled deeply. "B.O. for the butterfly orchid."

"Per Mom, natural is always best," I said. "Enjoy!" I flapped my arms to air them out and smiled.

"You might be smelling the plants I set around the tent to keep bugs, mosquitoes, and bad energy away. It's like a smudge." Gumbo held out a hand. "Begone, evil spirit! Negative energy, disappear!"

When Ellen and I exchanged confused looks, Gumbo said, "Never mind."

Even though he was different, Gumbo was gentle, kind, and caring. Bix was so cute that I wanted to take him home. And although Asha was aloof and often stared into space or shrubs, she was interesting. What a wacky group of peeps we made.

"I wish I had a survival kit," Ellen said. "We'll be out of drinking water by tomorrow."

"Yep," I said. "It would've been good to have water purification tablets, a compass, and—"

"Your cologne." Ellen bit her bottom lip, controlling her smile.

"I'm trying to be serious here!"

"Okay then, pimple cream."

I touched the bumps on my cheeks. "They're ant bites."

"They look nice in the moonlight," Bix said. "Like those stars." He pointed up.

Ellen giggled. "The Little Dipper."

"Thanks, Ellen. Thanks." I couldn't help it. I smiled superwide.

"Aw, two best friends." Bix smiled.

"We're not friends!" we said.

Bix jerked his neck back. "What?"

Nano held out a paw. "Don't ask."

When Gumbo angled his head to glance at us, his eyes glowed reddish orange against the moonlight. Creepy!

Bix crawled to the empty spot between Ellen and me and closed his eyes.

A chuck-will's-widow, not too far from us, started calling, "Darling, I'm here. Darling, I'm here. Darling, I'm here."

So that was what the annoying bird near our house said all night. But this time I noticed how his call affected the air, like sound waves or vibrational waves, reaching far across the Everglades. Maybe others of his kind could actually hear it or sense it. I closed my eyes to feel the air. In the distance, another bird of his kind sent a response, and maybe even a third one joined in the conversation. The call couldn't really be heard but felt deep within me. The sounds also reacted when they bounced off trees and objects. The weird part? Based on the vibrational changes, I could tell what those objects were. Cool.

"I need to lie down for a second," Ellen said with a yawn. She lay sideways and used her hands as a pillow.

As I gazed out in front of me, something strange was happening. I could almost see through the trees. Little red and orange shapes—animals—hid or crept in the woods. I shook my head. Maybe I was going crazy. I switched my focus to the stars and gazed at the Big and Little Dippers, pinpricks of light, wishing I'd studied how to navigate using the stars. Then Ellen would have been impressed and thought I was mature. Instead, I had the Little Dipper on my face.

I lay back and covered us with a thick layer of itchy palmetto fronds.

Thoughts about my parents bugged me again. Were they staring at the skies too? Were they here, right now, stuck like we were? Or were they in a hospital and hurt? Were they in Everglades City, meeting with the police and rescue people?

Ellen was sleeping soundly already. What if she lost her mom? Tears stung my eyes, and I brushed them away.

I tried to close my tired eyes, but they kept snapping open. I was afraid the night held dangers just waiting to sneak into our mini tent. I hadn't needed Gumbo or anyone to tell me that. Even the tiniest of creatures, like a mosquito carrying diseases, could kill us.

Through a small opening on the palmetto roof, I stared at the pasty white moon—beautiful, yeah, but it reminded me of monster movies. I shivered and deliberately closed my eyes.

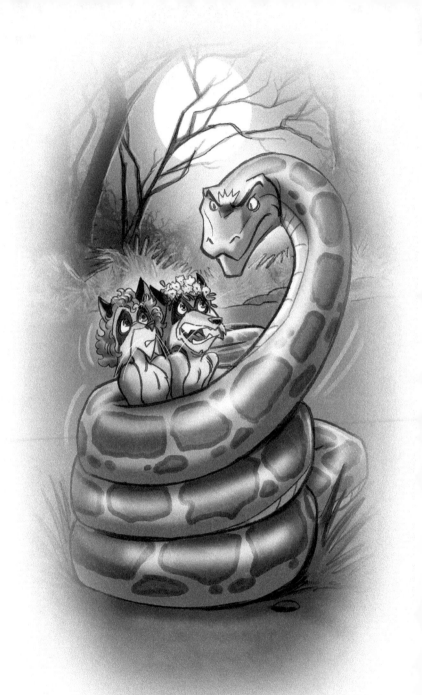

TWENTY

Reluctant Allies

 A haze crept over the luminous moon, and when it passed, the moon's color morphed into a blood red.

Louis, the mutant python, switched his gaze from the moon to the shrubs a few feet away, where he sensed the heat of two raccoons and a Norway rat. He slipped out his forked tongue, confirming the wispy scents, and when he was satisfied, he slithered without the slightest sound toward the shrubs.

In one blazing swoop, Louis trapped the raccoons, Peeka and Boo, with his elongated torso. He constricted their frail bodies in a leisurely fashion, just enough to wound but not enough to kill. After all, he needed them. For now.

Peeka's yellow flower toupee fell off and crumbled when it hit the ground. Boo's curls frizzed against Louis's musty breath. With every passing second, their eyes became more bloodshot, their breathing shallower. Death waited nearby.

Louis leaned near their faces.

"Tell me where a couple of young humans and a gator plan to go," Louis demanded silkily. Above his eyes, under the broad part of his head, he bore a mark in the shape of a crown.

"W-w-we don't—"

"—know anything."

Louis hissed. "I can smell them on you." He flicked out his tongue near Peeka's eyes.

"You're—"

"—mistaken."

"I'm ready to cook *ragout de raton laveur*—raccoon stew."

"They're searching for other humans," Peeka said.

"That's all we know!" Tufts of Boo's hair wiggled.

Louis released a long, impatient sigh like a king annoyed at his inferior subjects. "There once were raccoons who told a lie. They led two children to the river to die. They were later rewarded with a delicious pond apple pie."

Then Louis towered menacingly above their heads, blocking the pale moon and the icy stars from their view. "There once were raccoons who told no lie. They hid in the mangroves, thinking they could defy. They were later devoured. Oh poor little raccoons, goodbye." He hissed longer this time, frightening Peeka and Boo even more.

"Which poem do you like?"

"The latter. Uh, the former! The former!" Peeka quivered.

"Brain fart," Boo said.

"Find them and tell lies. Lead them to the widest section of the mangrove river." Louis released Peeka and Boo.

They tumbled to the ground, snapped their bones back into place, and streaked away without daring to look back.

Louis watched his reluctant allies disappear. Then he felt the vibrations of a distant motor through his skin, traveling to his muscles and into his inner ear. They reminded him of a luxury truck from long ago.

His wicked expression transformed into a child's priceless innocence as he recalled another night, a night when the tires of a truck crunched gravel as it crawled along a dirt road in an Everglades pine forest.

Cashmere had covered young Louis's golden cage. Inside, he wondered with dread where they were taking him. Though a few months old, he had grown abnormally fast to twelve feet, and so he coiled his muscles tightly in the cramped cage and gnawed his heart-shaped chew toy to calm himself.

The truck stopped.

When the driver stepped out, he hurried toward the rear of the truck, opened the tailgate, and lowered young Louis's cage to the ground.

Unable to see what was happening, young Louis trembled. This was not his comfortable home where he lived with eighteen-year-old Hugh La Ogé and his parents—the mom, a French chef; the dad, a wealthy businessman. Louis loved the mom and Hugh, but not the dad who had given him painful injections since he was a baby.

The cashmere lifted, and the taillights blinded young Louis for a second. A full moon eerily illuminated slash pines, saw palmettos, and other tropical shrubs on either side of the dirt road.

Louis dropped his chew toy, cringing at the sleek alligator boots in front of his cage. Mr. La Ogé threw down a cigar stub and crushed it.

Silhouetted in the truck, Hugh waited in his seat, but then he stuck his head out the window, his blond hair pearly white against the moonlit night.

"Dad, please. I want to take care of him. I'll bring him to college with me. He should be fine in my condo."

Mr. La Ogé shushed his son, then unlocked the cage and pointed to the exit. "Go on, Louis, you'll make friends out here. There's plenty of rats to eat. Remember the *rattus à la bordelaise* you learned to cook yesterday?" He mimicked a vile, greedy rat—teeth gnashing, hands wringing, eyes leering—perfectly. "It tasted good, didn't it? I promise we'll visit you." He tried to reassure him with a nod and a fake porcelain grin.

Steadily, almost cautiously, young Louis slithered out, but when Mr. La Ogé stepped forward, he flashed out like a football player dodging a tackle.

In record speed, Mr. La Ogé packed the cage and drove off, leaving a trail of dust clouds.

Waving goodbye, Hugh watched the tearful face of his pet from his side-view mirror.

Young Louis whimpered and cried, left for dead in a foreign land. What had he done wrong? Was he not worthy of love? He'd thought Hugh and his mom loved him in return. But he must have been mistaken.

When haunting sounds of animals closed in around him, his sadness changed to fear. Glowing eyes randomly appeared, blinking in and out. Hearing a deep growl, he yelped and fled into the night.

Louis's eyes watered at the memory of being thrown away like a used cigar.

Then he hissed and slapped the nearby shrubs, angry at himself for being weak. *I hate humans.* Now he had a chance to murder two: a revenge kill to wrap cashmere around his wounded heart. He'd almost had the boy, the one with similar hair and eye color to Hugh. He vowed that next time there'd be no escape.

In the distance, the faint call of a chuck-will's-widow echoed in the quiet night. Louis narrowed his eyes, sensing the bird's vibrations. He turned his head toward the maddening call and slithered into the darkness.

TWENTY-ONE

Change Our Plans

At dawn, nature's rituals persisted: the gray catbird meowed inside a saw palmetto, the mockingbird crooned on a branch, the pileated woodpecker drummed against a pine tree. For Asha and me, we practiced breathing exercises and meditation, followed by hatha yoga, and then finished again with meditation. We performed this every day at sunrise and sunset.

Now the life-giving sun rose, and soon the foggy mist coating the landscape would burn off along with the morning dew droplets dotting a spiderweb, a mosquito who blinked at me, and the stringy hairs on Nano's ears.

Nano snuck out from under the saw palmetto leaves and tinkled. He kicked sand to cover the area behind him, completely missing the spot by several inches.

I rose and stretched, my joints popping, then froze midpose. Cobwebs littered the landscape on shrubs, on saw palmettos, on tree branches—everywhere! My face broke into spasms.

Asha stepped right in front of me.

"See with spirit eyes?" I asked, anticipating her wisdom.

"You have eye boogers in buckets," she said. "I'm not vision challenged."

I rubbed my eyes clean.

Still fast asleep, Ocean and Ellen must have been exhausted physically and mentally. Bix nestled between their faces, snoring with a quiet *hoot* every few seconds.

The mockingbird started to mimic various birds.

"Mockingbird, sir, can you help me with something, please?" I whispered. He swiftly flew away. I moved toward the gray catbird, still meowing. He flitted off before I reached him. High atop a pine, I waved to the red-bellied woodpecker, who hopped sideways, gradually moving out of view. Finding a bird to help us wasn't going to be easy with me around.

Once the sun displayed gallantly above the horizon, blue jay warriors, about five of them, screamed at each other from several trees, asking where the hawks were hiding and where they could find food. I waved to the blue jays, and when they saw me, they screamed in quick succession, "Danger! Danger! Danger!" All kinds of birds hightailed it from our area as if escaping a hawk.

Ocean and Ellen roused from slumber. With eyes still closed, they turned toward each other, and their lips touched Bix's nose, which saved them from accidentally kissing each other. They blushed and sprang apart.

"Good morning!" they said.

"Namaste." I bowed.

"Nature calls," Ocean said groggily, heading toward the saw palmetto shrubs.

Ellen disappeared in another direction.

"What is nature calling about?" Bix asked.

Nano whispered the answer, yet he still looked baffled.

Bix approached me and waved to the morning sun.

"I love today! It's going to be a great day!" Bix sang his favorite song every morning.

> *The sun warms my face.*
>
> *The rain tickles my nose.*
>
> *It doesn't matter what the weather holds,*
>
> *'Cause I'm gonna have a great day.*
>
> *I swim to first place.*
>
> *I can bumble the race.*
>
> *It doesn't matter if I win or lose,*
>
> *'Cause I'm gonna have a great day.*
>
> *I feel terrific! I feel amazing!*
>
> *I'm going to give my smile to everyone*
>
> *I meet and greet today!*
>
> *Today, today is a very special day.*
>
> *Today, today is going my way.*
>
> *It's one of a kind.*
>
> *It's here, then it's gone.*
>
> *And so I'm going to make today the best day ever!*

After Bix finished singing and dancing, I said to Ocean and Ellen, "I know where we've been, so we can continue looking for the airboat in other sections near waterways. Does that work for you?"

"That's good, Gumbo," Ellen said. "Thanks for taking the lead."

Ocean grinned at Ellen. "Agreed. Show us the way!"

I wished they didn't give so much credence to my navigational abilities. Or anything else from me for that matter.

We trooped toward a marsh next to a sodden bayhead tree island with patches of pond apple trees. The fruits provided a bit of liquid and some sustenance even though they had a lot of seeds to sift through and weren't fully ripe.

"Would you like more pond apples?" I held out two.

Ocean spat out the seeds. "No thanks. I'm already struggling to keep what I have in my stomach from coming back up as a smoothie."

I learned new things from my friends. Smoothie, a word for vomit.

As we traipsed onward, two peculiar raccoons, smelling of human perfume, joined us.

Ocean and Ellen had already met them. While we were introduced, they kept checking the bushes, running in and out. Not sensing any danger, I didn't understand their anxious demeanor.

Ellen stepped closer to them. "Do you have another map? We lost the one we had."

A sprouting plant occupied the top of Peeka's head. Boo's hair stuck out in rigid spikes, the tips highlighted in rainbow colors.

"Want some pond apples?" Ocean asked. "We have a boodle of them."

They shook their heads stiffly, their eyes wide. Boo scratched his head at the word *boodle*.

"We don't—" Peeka said.

"—have a map," Boo said with a British accent.

"But we can tell you—"

"—the jiffy way to go."

"Make sure to continue straight through—"

"—a mossy hammock forest, just a hop, skip, and a jump away."

"Then across a mixed marsh and through a large bayhead tree island—"

"—then the marl prairie before the widest part of the mangrove river."

Peeka and Boo exchanged furtive glances.

"May I ask why that specific route?" There were many ways to get there, and these two brothers were odd. Something didn't sit right about their manner.

"You have a good chance to see other humans—"

"—only if you go that exact way."

"Then if you make it out a—" Boo stared at Peeka, and Peeka continued, "Then if you make it, you'll find something—"

"—or someone at the mangrove river."

"There's plenty of—"

"—blokes and big things."

"Yeah, big."

They giggled.

"Is it very far from here?" Ocean asked in a British accent.

"No."

"Not far."

"Brilliant!" Ocean said. "Do you want to join us?"

"No—"

"—thanks."

"Any more—"

"—nut bars?"

"Sorry, mate, only two left, and I can't spare them. When I return someday, I'll be sure to bring you some. Cheerio!"

"How about a—"

"—cell phone exchange?" Boo pulled out a cell phone from somewhere.

Where had he kept it? Never mind. I didn't want to know.

"Let me see it first."

Boo gave it to Ocean, who quickly wiped it with the bottom of his shirt.

Ellen leaned over as Ocean tried to turn it on. From what I could gather, it didn't belong to their parents. It didn't have phone service. And it didn't have much battery life. That may not be a good barter.

Ocean said to Ellen, "Maybe we can post a quick video, and Peeka and Boo can give it to any humans they see later."

"All right, let's do it fast." Ellen stepped away to give him space.

Ocean held the cell phone at arm's length and began speaking about their situation. Wanting to see what he was looking at, I snuck in next to him and accidentally bumped his ear with my big snout, so he introduced all of us. Perhaps we were the reason he didn't have enough time to provide his home address before the battery died.

Ellen shook her head and said, "Unbelievable."

"They can search our names online and in the news." Ocean returned the phone to Boo. He split a bar in two and gave it to the raccoons.

"We'll be sure to—"

"—give it to a human," Boo said.

"How did you meet each other?" I asked.

"I caught them trying to kiss Ellen." Ocean smiled.

"No, they weren't trying to do that." Ellen frowned and shook her head.

The raccoons giggled.

"Onward to the wide mangrove river! *Beep. Beep. Beep. Bop.*"

Ellen jumped next to Ocean. "We have to find the airboat."

Ocean opened an imaginary book. "Let's see. We don't know where it is, check. We're out of drinking water, check. We're out of food, check. We only have today—a very special day—to get help or we're dead, check. There might be people at the mangrove river. *Ding, ding, ding.*"

"No! We need to find our parents!"

"We tried. We don't know where they are. Besides, I have a feeling our parents are safe. They're probably in better shape than we are right now."

"You don't know that for sure." Ellen sounded tearful.

"Well, it's better than"—Ocean stiffened his body as though he were inside the python—"Snakezilla turning our bodies into protein shakes." He pointed to Nano. "And using Nano as a squeak toy!"

Nano trembled and yelped, "Eek!"

"What about me?" Bix asked.

"Stewed turtle."

"I bet I taste good." Bix grinned.

Before I could say anything, Ocean added, rather maturely, "If we go to the river—together—we might have a chance to run into people. We have to change our plans. It doesn't mean we're giving up on our parents. We're still looking for them, but *as* we're going to the river. Trust me, I'm just as worried as you are."

Ellen blinked a few times, fending off tears.

"Remember Gumbo's advice?" Ocean said. "Let's visualize our parents in a chopper, finding us at the river."

I visualized myself at the river too, with Father hugging me and telling me how proud he was of me despite losing both awards.

"I guess the rescue people might find us easier in an open area and maybe even kayakers might come down the river, right?" Ellen asked, staring at Ocean and me.

I gave her a smile that didn't reach my eyes, hoping she didn't notice.

Nano said, "Onward."

"Right! Now let's head to the mangrove river. *Beep, beep, bop.*"

"Good one for your dad," Bix said, pointing to a small python escaping into the tree island.

"No time for that, Bix," I said, then mumbled, "Not ever."

We continued our hike, and not long after that, we arrived at the edge of the jungle-covered hammock forest.

My senses lit up. We shouldn't go in there.

TWENTY-TWO
Like an Animal

"Let's go in," I said. "Peeka and Boo said this was the way. There might be people hiking. And it looks interesting." Yeah, interesting if I wanted to fall on a rattler or trip and break my neck.

Ellen said, "Gumbo?"

Gumbo was rolling one wrist bead after another.

Not waiting for his response, I forged ahead. At this point, it was midmorning, and I wouldn't mind some shade anyway.

Different than the last tree island with the spider, this one had Spanish moss draping hardwood trees, creeping vines crawling through other plants, and dead fallen tree trunks littering the ground. Vines ate up one tree all the way to the top. I hadn't realized that a friendly competition simmered among plant life for space, light, and water.

I also felt we were intruders—the bad guys. I tipped my head back, studying the mature trees. Through their roots, the trees warned each other that we were here. As we hiked, I could feel them watching our every move, afraid of what we'd do. Weird how I could sense that, but hey, I was a tree in my dream.

Once again I smelled the river otter, like I smelled him at the haunted tree island. Either his musky scent had stuck on me like glue, or he was following us. I sped ahead.

A stifled sneezing in the shrubs spooked us, making us bunch together while we quickened our pace. Gumbo mingled a bit too close for my taste. All I saw were his nostrils and teeth over my shoulders. Not pretty. He got the hint and stepped back.

In front of us, a shrub rustled. When we stopped, the rustling also stopped. Next to it stood a sculpture of a deer made from twigs, branches, and vines. To my right, another deer sculpture, this one with his head down on the grass, and to my left, a deer sleeping. We must have stumbled into someone's home. I didn't have time to figure out whose because another plant ahead of us rocked as though something intended to jump out. We had to get our butts out of there.

We sprinted as fast as we could while high jumping, side jumping, and zigzagging to avoid tripping hazards.

After a few minutes of sprinting, we stopped to catch our breath. A baritone growl sounded from within a flowering shrub, raising the hair on my neck. I was already stepping away when suddenly a squirrel scampered out and climbed the nearest tree, screaming and flicking his tail.

"Stay away! Stay away!" he yelled. Once he reached the highest branch, he leaped to another tree.

Ellen and I laughed. I'd forgotten how ominously squirrels could growl.

But when a shadow emerged to our left, I felt the blood drain from my face.

Framed against a tree on a low branch, the same skinny panther who'd scared us on the airboat glowered, just as he had before. His eyes smoldered like twin greenish-gold stones.

"What are you, deaf?" he roared.

With my left hand covering my right finger pointing at Asha, I whispered, "She is a bit."

Asha eyeballed me.

The panther inched forward along the branch and snarled. "Get out of my land!"

"Okay!" Ellen spun around and took off running.

Oh no!

"A gamer!" The panther ran after her.

Bix clapped. "I want to play."

I helplessly watched as they whizzed from one tree to the next. Ellen moved as swiftly and fluidly as the panther. She definitely had new physical abilities.

What should I do? I had to come up with a plan. It wouldn't make sense for the panther to chase us both.

Just then the panther pounced toward Ellen. She sidestepped behind a tree. The panther tumbled and crashed into a shrub and shot out instantly. Ellen and the panther disappeared beyond a cluster of trees.

I checked behind me to see what the others were doing. Asha's left wing gyrated uncontrollably, and she plunged backward. After Gumbo helped her up, he shuffled in

Ellen's direction and tripped. Bix blasted from Gumbo's shoulder into a thicket.

"Sorry!"

"I'm fine!" Bix said.

Okay, they might not be helpful.

Think, Ocean. Think.

Gathering as much hanging moss and as many branches as I could hold, I sprinted through the hardwood forest, searching for Ellen and the panther.

They headed to an area covered with fallen and rotted trees. I ran ahead of them, without them seeing me, and climbed to the top of a leaning tree, where I got myself ready and in position to peer through a veil of hanging vines and moss.

Ellen weaved between shrubs and trees like it was an obstacle course, the panther still racing behind her. Then he veered off in a new direction.

Where did he go?

"Miss me?" The panther casually leaned against a tree in front of Ellen.

Ellen shrieked in surprise.

She flung a branch at him. He dodged it. She pointed her walking stick. He took it, splintering it to shreds. She chucked sand into his eyes.

"Ouch! You don't play fair." He wiped his eyes and scanned the area. Ellen had already moved on. He sniffed the air.

To my left, Gumbo scrambled toward the panther and nose-dived into some bushes. He should run on all fours in this bumpy section.

Ellen skittered to a cluster of thick trees close to me and clambered up. I wasn't sure if that was the best option. Should I go out there now or wait for my plan to unfold?

Below her, the panther said, "Really? You know I can climb trees, right?"

She reached the broadest part of a limb and searched the ground.

Gumbo came out of the bushes, rubbing his head.

"Give up." The panther swung from a vine in front of Ellen.

She grabbed vines and leaves to buffer her fall, then she dove and tumbled into dense foliage and rolled out. Nano surfaced from the carrier, blinking nonstop. They were almost to me. My plan had better work.

The panther landed right behind her.

Below me, Ellen slid under a clump of fallen trees just as the panther swooped toward her.

The four tree trunks protected her like a cage with narrow openings at the bottom and a few smaller ones at the top. Overgrown weeds and ferns lined the trees.

The panther flexed his sharp claws, stretching and reaching into the opening between the ground and a tree trunk.

I moved out from cover.

"*Grraaah.* You get out of *my* land!" With my arms raised and palm fronds in both hands, tree branches hooked to my pants, and moss covering me, I towered over the panther. I hoped I looked like a scary blond skunk ape.

The panther fell back, his ribs noticeable on his skinny body.

Gumbo—just ten feet from the panther—gawked at me. Asha carried Bix and showed up next to him.

Ellen and Nano watched through an opening between two tree trunks.

I unwrapped my last nut bar and threw it to the panther. "*Grraaah.* Take it and go!"

The panther picked up the snack with his teeth and munched hungrily as he fled.

"Ellen!" I removed the itchy moss and jumped down.

From under the trees, she kicked her way out.

"Are you and Nano okay?" I asked. *Yikes.* Huge bugs were crawling all over her shirt and long hair. "You have some dirt on you," I said while slapping the critters off.

"Yes, thank you, Ocean." She couldn't take her eyes off me. She dusted herself off, tilted her head, and blinked several times.

Nano said, "Thanks! Brave!"

Bix, Gumbo, and Asha joined us. Gumbo grinned at me. I wasn't used to all those teeth.

"I loved the costume, Ocean," Bix said. "Wasn't that fun?"

"Bix, ever hear of stranger danger?" Ellen asked.

"No."

"Strangers can be dangerous," Ellen said. "Never, ever talk to them even if they pretend to be nice or hurt or need your help. Always call an adult immediately."

"Oh, but I want to be their friend."

Nano pointed to Bix. "Snack."

Ellen's right arm was bleeding.

"You're hurt!" I said.

She moved her arm away. "It's just a scratch."

Yeah, right—blood was literally dripping. What should I do?

While she wiped the blood with tissues, I circled her like a nervous mother duck. We didn't have a first aid kit, something else I needed to remember to take with me when hiking the woods.

Gumbo examined her arm. With eyes closed, he hovered his right palm above the cut.

"Om. Healing energy, white light—or is it a blue light? Maybe it's a yellow light. Healing light surrounds you and heals your wound. Think health. Think all is well. Think clean and keep it clean." Then Gumbo said, "That was impressive, Ocean."

"Thanks, it was nothing," I said, then to Ellen, "You were running, jumping, and climbing just like an animal!"

She half smiled. "Yeah, it was awesome. I just did it without thinking. You know, out of all this mess, I really love having this talent. Remember we wished for it?"

"Yep." I felt we were friends again.

"But I don't like the smells."

I wondered if I smelled bad or not too bad. She had joked that I stank last night. I bent my head to sniff myself without being too obvious. Ah, the sweet scent of blueberry pie—not.

Ellen exhaled deeply. "Thanks, guys. Let's keep going. My arm is fine."

"Here, use this." I handed her my walking stick. "I'll make another one on the way. *Beep, beep, beep,* let's go!"

Ellen rolled her eyes, though this time she also smiled.

Interesting. Maybe I'd made a positive impression. I hoped so. The thought made me blush, so I focused on the path ahead.

Something was different. My feet felt light and airy, my surroundings seemed brighter and more beautiful, my head exploded with vibrant colors, and those colors expanded to everything.

I still had a chance to be her hero, so I visualized us alive and safe at the mangrove river. Ellen would be hugging me and telling me how much she'd missed me. Then our parents would arrive in a helicopter and take us home.

Yes, all of that would happen for sure. We could move mountains if we believed, right?

TWENTY-THREE

Dangling in a Gumbo

Though grateful to see the light ahead, signaling the end of our trip through the large hammock tree island, I continued monitoring for snakes along our path.

"Gumbo. Next time could you suggest the way to go, please?" Ellen said. "You know, so Ocean doesn't take us the wrong way?"

I clasped my wrist mala beads tightly and chanted in my mind. She was right, of course. I could have said something. I couldn't even save her from the panther.

"For the record," Ocean said, "that's where Peeka and Boo said to go."

Ellen gave Ocean a supportive smile. "It's okay. I would have done the same."

They eyed each other before turning away when their cheeks flushed. They had a connection, perhaps as soul mates.

Asha squinted at them as if to view their auras. I unfocused my eyes and stared at the area just next to their bodies, then half closed my eyelids to create a fuzzier vision so I could see hues of color around them. These colors supposedly showed their emotional state, yet I didn't see any auras. I was such a failure.

Be gentle with yourself.

Ellen peered at my downcast face and touched my shoulder. "You're smart, Gumbo, very smart. You can do anything. Just be confident, you know?" With a glint in her eye, she added, "On the other hand, Ocean is too confident when he shouldn't be." She snorted a laugh.

Ocean playfully hit her stick, and she hit back.

"Of course he's smart," Bix said, patting my head. "He knows a lot. Gumbo is the king's eldest son, and he'll be our next king!"

"The next king?" Ellen stopped walking. She sounded shocked.

"King Gumbo," Ocean said. "Eh, it could be worse. King Bumfuzzle. King Sneezewort."

"I like Sneezewort," Bix said.

"King Fartsalot." Ocean laughed. He did something with his hand and made a noise. Bix and Nano giggled.

I didn't want to think about being the king or about being brave anymore. "Can we shift our thoughts to something else?"

"How about some lunch?" a familiar voice said above us, sending chills through my body.

Bix said, "Lunch sounds good."

We all tilted our heads back to search the tree.

Draped languidly on a branch, dangling in a gumbo-limbo tree and controlling his spittle, the mutant python focused on a target—Ocean.

"Hi, Biggie Mouth!" Bix said. "Wait. Stranger danger?"

"Yes!" Nano yelled from inside Ellen's shaking pouch.

The python leaned forward, ready to inhale Ocean, and my knees buckled.

Ocean watched saliva drip onto his shirt. "Slurpee is back."

Despite the joke, his voice trembled. We wouldn't be able to move fast enough to avoid an attack.

"Too late to go," Asha said. Birds snapped out of trees and shrubs from her ear-piercing voice.

The python jerked in surprise. Without warning, the branches holding the python cracked, and he crashed down on us.

One jagged stem cut the mala beads from my wrist, scattering them in all directions. I cried out, unable to reach for them.

I lay motionless, my eyes glued to the brown diamond design on the python's skin, his dry scales and thick muscular torso pressing on me.

And my mind somersaulted back in time.

At four years old in a mixed swamp, I had been collecting herbs with Mother.

"Gumbo, my little darling, don't go off too far," she said. "I know how brave you are, but stay close, okay?"

"Okay, Mother."

While she searched for plants, I played next to a small pond, not far from her. A few minutes later I spotted a green frog and chased him past the pond, around a shrub, over some rocks—then caught him. The frog trembled under my grasp, so I set him free with apologies. I realized I'd strayed too far from Mother and raced back as fast as I could.

Once I reached the area near the pond, I parted a cluster of pickerelweed, their purple flowers blooming spectacularly during the wet summer.

Mother!

Two men carried Mother and dumped her on a swamp buggy. She had duct tape on her mouth, hands, and feet. I had to stop them! I jumped out to fight, but Mother saw me and shook her head. Her eyes warned me to stay away. I darted back behind the pickerelweed before the men saw me.

Mother's eyes watered as she watched me. I could sense her telling me she loved me.

I teared up. With my chest heaving, I let her read my eyes, which begged her to let me attack.

She lightly shook her head, and I felt the most painful words expressed in her face: *Goodbye, Gumbo.*

The men's laughter and comments about pitchers of beer and frog legs burned into me. They threw beer cans and wrappers out from the buggy, then roared off before Mother could give me a sign.

I chased after the buggy, and soon it was just ten feet away. Mother saw me and tried to move. Without warning, the tires splattered mud on my face, blinding me, and I slammed into a thicket and tumbled into a ditch right on top of several baby rat snakes, who immediately wrapped themselves around my body. I couldn't breathe. I couldn't move.

The babies practiced constricting me while I cried for Mother, not ceasing until the snake's mother arrived and shoved them away.

As I lay there panting and crying, hundreds of juvenile wolf spiders with their eight mothers swarmed and engulfed every part of my body except my two wet eyeballs. They bit and scratched until finally I screamed. That scattered them, so I crawled out, still trembling. To my dismay, the swamp buggy had disappeared. I ran and searched for her as long as I could.

But I never found Mother.

"Wake up, Gumbo!" Bix's young voice pierced my memories. His blurry face grew clear.

"All we have is now. There is no other time," Asha said.

I missed Mother so much. For two years we had searched until Father and my brothers gave up. Father blamed me for leaving her alone. My brothers blamed me for staying in the shrub. I blamed myself for all of the above. But deep within me, I still believed she was out there, somewhere, waiting for me to save her.

"Gumbo, please!" Ellen said. "We need you."

I glanced at Ocean and Ellen, barely registering our situation. They pushed the branch and the python's thick body without success.

The python's eyes flipped open.

Nano dug deeper into Ellen's pouch.

The python whipped his head around, a twisted smile spreading across his face.

My friends needed me! "I am here in the present."

I lifted the python and the branches and threw them over our heads, using the yoga plow pose. I rolled into a handstand and jumped to a standing pose while Bix swung wildly around my neck, clutching my mala beads.

Contorted around the branch in a ditch, the python looked stupefied. He raised his head in time to receive an onslaught of debris and plants hurtling from my tail. I bombarded him again before I helped Ocean and Ellen to their feet and scooped up Asha. We raced toward the river.

The python coughed out the dirt and grumbled, "Plan B," as he untangled himself and pulverized the branches around him.

He had a plan? Of course he did. He wasn't giving up. Another thought scared me: did he have kids? Pythons could lay eighty to a hundred eggs at a time. How many kids had he made over the years? Where were they? Would they grow just as large?

Father was right. If we didn't do something, they'd take over, and everyone, not just alligators, would be doomed.

TWENTY-FOUR

Thank You

We raced through the king-size tree island and out to a mixed marsh. We'd escaped for now. If not for Gumbo, Ellen and I would be dead. We weren't strong enough to push the python lying on us like a fallen elephant.

I thought about my parents again. Could they have escaped if he attacked? Probably not. He would get Mom first. Thinking about that kind of stuff wasn't helping me. I had to visualize and believe that my parents were safe and searching for us. They'd find us soon and bring gallons of water and my favorite veggie burger with sweet potato fries. Those thoughts made me feel better. Asha had mentioned to us that we didn't know the future anyway, so we might as well trust and believe it would turn out good. That made sense. Why ruin the day and make ourselves miserable for an unknown?

In sync, we all slowed down to pace ourselves. Gumbo released Asha, and Bix twirled on Gumbo's shoulder, steadying himself as he got bounced around.

"You got it, Gumbo!" Ellen said. "Thanks for saving us!"

Gumbo bowed with hands in prayer. He seemed a bit more confident, with his shoulders square instead of hunched over.

In an Indian accent, I said, "Gumbo, the yogi master. Namaste." I punched his shoulder, which felt like metal armor.

"I'll be adding all of you to my gratitude journal." Gumbo sang a thank-you song as we trekked through the mixed marsh lined with lots of wildflowers.

His song cheered me up. What had Meister Eckhart said that Dad shared with me? Something like *if the only prayer we ever said was thank you, it would be enough.* My parents—big on saying thank you—would get along well with Gumbo, Asha, and Bix. Too bad they'd never get a chance to meet our new friends.

I'd asked Asha before if we could keep Yaha's gift. She just stared at the trees. Maybe I should ask her again.

"Asha, will Yaha take back his gift for sure once we go home?"

Asha waved to a white orchid. We all stopped to view the rare ghost orchid. It had these delicate white petals and curly, larger ones beneath. It did look like a ghost and also an angel—and a fancy jacket for a lizard.

Well, she didn't say he would take it away, so we still had a chance to keep the gift.

"Hey, Nano, you see anything?" I pointed to the trees around us and the ghost orchid.

"No."

"Well, I'm thankful to Yaha," I said, "and I'm thankful to all of you."

While we traveled across the mixed marsh toward the bayhead tree island, I thought about Ellen.

Aside from saving us from danger, Gumbo and Asha made it easier for Ellen and me to get along. I snuck a side-glance at her. She still seemed dreamy about the ghost orchid. I felt the same. We both loved the same things, the same activities, the same people.

Gumbo pointed to an air plant attached to a cypress tree. He peeked inside the plant. "This large bromeliad still has water. You can drink from it."

Ellen and I rushed to the plant, licking our cracked lips in anticipation.

"I hope the water is clean." Ellen made a face.

"Just drink it. It's not pee," I said.

Anyway, it tasted fine. Even though there was only enough water for a few sips, it sure helped. We hadn't seen anything else to drink. Gumbo said there were coconuts, oranges, grapefruits, and other berries in the Everglades. Other than the yucky pond apple, we hadn't found such foods along our way. Maybe it wasn't the right season.

Finally we arrived at a large bayhead tree island a few yards away.

I sniffed the air, then myself. I smelled the otter and also the raccoons. Peeka and Boo didn't want to go to the river, so it couldn't be them. The idea of jumping into a warm shower and getting rid of otter slobber sounded wonderful.

As we headed toward a narrow opening, I noticed a sign—Hiking Trail—mounted with vines to a cypress tree. "Look over there." I pointed to it. "This must be where Peeka and Boo said to go through. After this, it's the open marl prairie and then the mangrove river." I glanced at Gumbo.

Gumbo paused for a second. "It might be best to stay on the outside."

"Will it take longer that way?" Ellen asked.

"Well, yes, but—" Gumbo grabbed his wrist. No beads there. He exhaled and faced Asha. "I am here in the present."

"Loving it!" Bix smiled.

Nano stared up at Ellen. "Careful."

Danger or not, we had to go through, and in reality, danger lurked everywhere anyway. The Everglades had teeth, claws, spears, and poison too.

With hardly any light filtering through the swamp, we stepped into ankle-deep water, which quickly rose to knee-high, then waist-high. The uneven ground felt nubby from roots crawling all over each other. Tall trees of all types surrounded us with their thick branches crisscrossing to create a bridge across their tops.

Growl.

Hissss.

Bellow.

Gators. Not good. We remained still. Gumbo could handle alligators, right? His dad was the king, so we were safe. Or so I hoped.

Alligator heads surfaced, one by one, until thirty or more surrounded us.

"Blend in," I whispered. "*Growl, hissss, bellow.*"

Ellen slipped next to me as she half smiled at my joke. She probably thought Gumbo could save us as I did.

Bix clapped. "You sound just like them!" He turned to the gators and waved. "Hello! Sorry to bother your nappy time."

Ellen's carrier rocked wildly. "Stranger danger!" Nano yelped.

"Oh." Bix jerked his head back into his shell, his tubular nose still visible.

"Namaste." Gumbo bowed. "I'm the son of our king. You know, the powerful one." He laughed nervously. Then he bowed with his hands in prayer and fidgeted, stirring up waves.

The gators near him submerged to watch his dancing feet, so he stopped.

A big alligator glided forward. He looked pretty old—and hungry.

"I know who you are," he said and pointed to a few nearby tree trunks that had carvings of an alligator dancing in a ballerina skirt.

A few gators giggled.

Was that supposed to be Gumbo? Not nice.

"I'm Aponi Fume, the elder of this cypress tribe."

"Hello, a pony for me," Bix said. "Not a stranger anymore?"

"Still!" Nano's ears vibrated from the edge of the carrier.

"We're just passing through, searching for other humans. Did you happen to see any recently?" Gumbo asked.

"Maybe I saw them, maybe I didn't," Aponi said, eyeing Nano's trembling ears. "I'll know better after your little friends join us for a dip."

"No!" Ellen covered her carrier.

"Nah, we're good," I said with a wink. "Go back to your nap or whatever you were doing under the water. It'll be our little secret." I slipped next to Nano and Ellen to protect them.

Gumbo made himself a few inches taller, and in a deep voice we hadn't heard before, he said, "Sorry. My friends can't give you a pony."

He was actually joking. Yesterday he couldn't have done that.

Asha laughed, and the water rolled into waves as if a T. rex were charging toward us. A couple of branches cracked and fell. Seriously, her voice could be used as a weapon.

Aponi tossed his head and growled.

"Love your name," Bix said and began to sing. "*A pony for me. A pony for you. A pony for us. A pony to ride.*" He still didn't get stranger danger.

The situation was this: they wouldn't kill Gumbo, but they'd kill Asha, Bix, and Nano. Then they'd chomp on Ellen and me to see if we were edible. Even if we were Gumbo's friends, it wouldn't matter to hungry gators, and with that many surrounding us, Gumbo couldn't stop them all. I had to think of something quick.

Behind me, a broad tree leaned against another, its trunk leading up to the treetops.

I pointed to a massive tree. "I saw several owls looking out from the hole in that tree. We can get them for you. Those owls should hold you over. I'm sure you don't want to harm Gumbo's friends. What would the king say?"

Ellen and Gumbo glanced up, catching my drift to escape up the tree.

The alligators gazed up and grumbled. At least they weren't jumping us yet.

"Look, I'll show you." I climbed up the leaning tree, and Ellen followed directly behind me.

Gumbo carried Asha and gave Aponi a fake smile as he hurried up the tree. He lost his footing on the slippery algae and almost fell sideways, but he leveled himself and continued toward the top.

"*A pony for me. A pony for you. A pony for us. A pony to ride.*"

"Namaste," Gumbo said with a bow to Aponi.

Aponi motioned to two muscular alligators, who then followed us.

Once I scaled the tree, I inspected the hole where I'd claimed to have seen owls. A corn snake, curled up inside, raised his head, and I whispered, "It's okay. Go back to sleep."

"Waiting!" Aponi yelled.

"Nothing here. Oh well, see ya later! Like never!" I tried to imitate their bellow. "Me hungry. Not too smart when hungry."

The branch I stood on cracked, and I went airborne.

"Ocean!" Ellen screamed.

I caught a handful of vines and thin branches. "I can handle it."

Five alligators below me roared straight out of the water, and I tucked in my legs as I dangled precariously. The vines dipped a bit. I might become alligator food.

A tree branch bent my way—Gumbo was pressing it down; his whole body shook with effort.

Just as the vines ripped loose from the tree, I grabbed the branch. When Gumbo released his hold, I flew in the air, moving my arms and legs as if doing an Olympic long jump, then I smacked into a tree.

"Ocean, you hurt?" Ellen asked.

"Yeah," I mumbled.

"Where?"

"In a spot that rhymes with Sasquatch." Well, sort of. Close enough to crotch.

Gumbo shattered a connecting branch to prevent the two gators from crossing. The fractured pieces fell, knocking several alligators in the head.

"Sorry! Blessings! Sending healing energy!"

The two muscular alligators just behind us moved back, priming for a leap.

I repeated the lyrics of Bix's song from this morning, "I feel terrific! I feel amazing!" I rose and staggered toward Ellen.

At the same time, the two alligators rocketed into the air, reaching for Gumbo.

Without hesitation, Gumbo swung a thick branch and thumped them really hard. They dropped like boulders, smashing those below who hadn't moved out of the way. Aponi attacked them, and they rolled around in the water.

"Sorry! Think health. Love and light!" Gumbo gestured wildly with his hands and probably a bit too much because his foot slipped. He wobbled and began to free-fall. He flung Bix to Asha, right before he plummeted.

She caught Bix in her wings.

On the same branch, Ellen seesawed too. Her arms windmilled to steady her swaying body. It wasn't enough. She plunged backward!

"Ellen!"

She landed safely, cushioned by Gumbo's belly. *Phew.*

Nano shot out of the carrier and bounced off one alligator then another, like a Ping-Pong ball, finally coming to rest on the back of a third. Tail tucked under his legs, he trembled uncontrollably.

Before I could move, Gumbo hugged Ellen tightly, dashed atop the alligators as though they were stepping-stones, and grabbed Nano right before a gator snapped his jaws. They disappeared beyond the shallow area, and I finally took in a long, shaky breath.

Asha handed me Bix, and I placed him safely in my pants pocket. She waved her feathers at me to follow her.

How could she always stay so calm with all the chaos and near-death situations?

Bix smiled. "A pocket with a view."

And Bix—always happy no matter what.

Then there was Gumbo. He'd saved our lives twice. Even though he was a scary gator, he was kind and had these regal, striking yellow-gold eyes.

"Let them go," Aponi said to his tribe. "It's best if temptations are gone. We'll find others who aren't Gumbo's friends."

As they glared at Asha and me, the alligators whined.

We'd survived again. I wondered what would have happened if that leaning tree hadn't been there. Maybe Gumbo would have threatened them. Or maybe he would have grabbed Aponi and made the rest of them beg for mercy.

Nope. Gumbo couldn't do that. Although after he lifted that python away and prevented gators from killing us, I felt that maybe in a year or two he could. He just lacked confidence, as Ellen had said.

Right now, with my insides crunchy, I worried about Ellen. Being separated wasn't good. She was right again.

TWENTY-FIVE
Holy Mud

Fifteen minutes passed. Twenty. Yet it felt like an hour. Ellen and I nervously waited fifty or more feet from the edge of Aponi's tribe, behind thin cypress trees. The spot provided the best position to see the others coming out from either end. Silently I prayed for their safety and well-being. If they didn't show up soon, we'd have to go back in.

"Do you think they're okay?" Ellen asked for the third time.

"It takes time to cross from tree to tree."

Her eyes glistened with unconcealed pain. They had only each other right now, just as I had only Asha and Bix.

"Ellen!" Ocean sprinted toward us from the dense trees, a bit lopsided from his loose sneakers, then he tripped facedown. Trailing right behind him, Asha hurried to help him back up.

When he finally reached us, he leaned forward as though about to hug Ellen, but instead, he dusted himself off and combed his hair using his fingers.

"Thank you," Nano barked at Ocean with arms outstretched.

Ellen handed him over, and Ocean kissed his round forehead.

Nano touched Ocean's face, and said, "Brave." Then he pointed at me and said the same.

I wasn't sure if I deserved that. Grabbing Ellen and Nano hadn't been brave. It was instinctive, something anyone would have done. Now, Ocean and Ellen? They were brave. I wished I were more like them.

"Thank you, Ocean, for thinking of an escape," I said. "You're resourceful."

"Yes!" Bix said from Ocean's pants pocket.

Ocean pulled him out and placed him on my shoulder. "Glad we're all okay, and thanks, Gumbo, for saving Ellen and Nano."

Ellen beamed at Ocean. "Thank you too. That was ingenious."

Ocean's face lit up.

"We'd better get moving," I said, anxious to get far from Aponi's tribe.

"Lead the way, King Gumbo," Ocean said with a smile.

Although this area wasn't under water, it was muddy. As I stepped ahead, squelching through the soggy ground, the suction noises from my feet and their shoes gradually became noisier as it got wetter.

Ocean made sounds using his hand but in a rhythmic beat with the suction noises. Bix giggled.

Suddenly a helicopter hummed in the distance.

"Let's get out of—" Ocean started to say.

"We can't move!" Ellen yelped.

Stuck in muddy quicksand—Holy Mud, the locals called it—Ocean and Ellen were sinking deeper by the second.

"We'll help you get unstuck," I said.

With her back to us, Asha was tying vines together. She twisted around and threw one end at them while holding the other.

A small green snake, mistakenly knotted to the vine, screamed.

Ocean and Ellen panicked, dipping down farther.

"Open your eyes wide," I said to Asha.

Asha's eyes widened. "Sorry," she said, gently untying the scared snake. "My bad. Droopy eyelids." She stretched her eyelids way out and snapped them.

Bix clapped.

"You have the tools," I said to Ocean and Ellen, pointing to their walking sticks. "Let me show you." I pretended to bend over with an imaginary walking stick, leaning my upper body forward and using the stick to grab some ground to crawl myself out.

"It works the adominoes," Bix said.

He meant the abdominals.

"Never mind. It's faster if you take my tail."

Just as I wheeled around, Ocean and Ellen shrieked.

"Stranger danger!" Bix yelled.

"Baddies!" Nano growled.

Two alligators from Aponi's tribe attacked Ocean and Ellen, who fought them using their walking sticks.

I wasn't certain of my next move.

"Poke them in the eye!" Ocean said.

Ocean knew an animal's sensitive spot. If an alligator seized a human's body part such as an arm, they should hurt the alligator's eyes. He might let go. Trying to pull the arm out or stretch our strong jaws apart was futile.

Asha twirled her walking stick, then lunged into warrior II, jabbing one alligator in the eye. She swung again, we all ducked, and she slapped the other gator.

"Be still!" I said to the gators.

Everyone paused. The gators blinked nonstop, their eyes watering.

"Go back now or face the consequences—blindness. I can also report you to my father, and your whole tribe might be expelled from the Everglades."

The alligators exchanged defeated looks and hissed all the way back out.

Once again I presented my tail to Ocean and Ellen. Ocean grabbed it; Ellen grabbed Ocean's pants. Finally they crawled out. Ocean's pants slipped below his bottom, and the mud ate his shoes and socks.

Ellen grinned. "Superman tighty-whities."

"I don't wear underwear," Bix said proudly.

Ocean's cheeks tinged red—on his face, not his buttocks. He quickly lifted his pants and underwear.

We set off toward an area where sparser cypress trees sprinkled the landscape.

"Why don't you fly over the trees with your Superman undies?" Ellen said with a smile.

"Why don't you fly over the trees with your broomstick?"

I was grateful to see them joking and seeming much more relaxed.

At the clearing, Ocean and Ellen jumped and hollered at the retreating chopper, now a freckle in the sky. All we could do now was pray for its return.

"They'll be back," Ocean said.

Ellen faced him. "Tell me the truth."

"Yes, you're starting to look like Nano." He laughed.

She and Nano glowered.

"Okay. You don't look like a kangaroo in that outfit."

Ellen sighed. "Do you really know your way to the river from here?"

"*Beep, beep.*" Ocean pointed away from the river. "Right, Gumbo?"

"It's actually more that way. We've been getting off track. We're better now."

"Exactly," Ocean said. "That way. King Gumbo, why don't you lead again?"

Ellen's frown melted. "Thanks."

Yesterday, Ocean had been adamant about leading even when he hadn't known the way. Since this morning, he seemed more cooperative and allowed me to take charge.

I wouldn't have led them before; however, now I felt I could. The timing was perfect for us both.

"Look, Gumbo. Another chance," Bix said.

Partially obscured by a tall shrub, a ten-foot Burmese python with a sizable lump in his stomach lay motionless.

Cyp and Will jumped out from the same shrub, and Cyp grabbed the python's neck and said, "Got you! Hee-hee, another easy catch."

"I smell dander," Will said. "And humans, a wood stork, a softshell turtle—and Gumbo!"

They both whirled around and spotted us.

Cyp sneered, "Well, if it isn't scaredo, dumbo, and weirdo."

"Oh, oh, which one am I?" Bix wondered.

"Why are you with humans? You better not be cheating or I'll tell Father," Cyp said.

Because I said nothing, Bix answered for me, "We're helping—"

"I wasn't talking to you, dumbo," Cyp said to Bix. Then he threw a branch toward my head.

I deflected it using one arm.

My brothers did a double take.

Usually I was too distraught and tense, so I'd get hit. Not this time. I stood firmly, eyeing them with my snout lifted. Standing up to them felt empowering and liberating. Asha was right again. What they said had nothing to do with me but everything to do with who they were. She had also said they sought love and compassion, which I didn't see at all, although she was always right.

"Ever hear of deep-fried gator nuggets?" Ocean glared at them. "I read they taste like fishy chicken. Maybe I want to find out if that's true."

Will cringed behind Cyp, whereas I gagged.

"Why are your words as clear as if you're speaking our language?" Cyp narrowed his eyes. "What sort of voodoo is going on here?"

"Yaha," Asha said.

"Zip it!" Cyp glared at Asha.

"Don't you ever talk to my friends like that again." Ellen stepped next to me. "Ever hear of the Golden Rule?"

"Oh, I know this one," Bix said. "So, you like to bully others, so that means you like others to bully you too."

"Also, like a boomerang, what you do to others will be done to you," Asha said. "It's karma, baby."

Cyp glared at Asha. "I have to take this Burm before he regains energy, so you lucked out." He flung the python over his shoulder and left with Will.

"Aw, thank you. Next time you'll luck out!" Bix yelled.

"Chicken nuggets!" Nano barked.

Ocean opened his palm to me, so I rested my forehead on his hand for his blessing.

He laughed. "No, I was trying to high-five you. Like this."

He raised my hand high and slapped it. Strange customs these humans had.

"You did good, Gumbo." Ellen winked at me and said to Ocean, "You too."

"I learned from the best. Ellen used to stand up to the bullies in my neighborhood."

I could see Ellen doing that. Even though she had let Ocean lead, she too was a leader and a strong yet kind human. Through our travels, she'd marched in step with him. While building the tent, she tied the palmettos over the branches and swept the ground perfectly. During the panther chase, she was not only fast and agile but also smart to elude him.

Ocean patted my back. "Behind Gumbo! *Beep, beep.*"

Ellen put her hand on her head, making the mapdar gesture as if it were out of control.

"I saw that." For Nano and Bix, Ocean exaggerated the mapdar hand movements, and the little ones laughed as they tried to imitate him.

At least the mood elevated even more on our last stretch. Perhaps it was optimism from being close to our goal and transcending the obstacles along our path. Or perhaps just like Bix, it was Ocean's natural affinity for joy, an admirable trait since this world was an illusion anyway, as Asha had told me many times.

Sadly, I couldn't feel the same lightness. What would happen once Ocean and Ellen were saved? What would I do? I hadn't caught or killed a single python. Father would be disappointed again, and everyone in the Everglades would laugh at me. A sense of failure lowered my energy. I suddenly felt tired.

I'd also miss Ocean and Ellen. They'd become close friends. There had to be a reason for all that we'd gone through together. Yet I had no clue what it could be. Asha said our meeting was destiny. The only destiny I'd known since I was a child was to be the next king.

But that would never happen because killing a python was not in my forecast.

TWENTY-SIX

Trippydy Tripp

In the wide area by a river, on the corner dotted with red mangrove trees, a river otter hugged his young sister. He released her and tenderly wiped the nut-bar crumbs from her furry little chin. His name was Tripp, the otter who'd tried to steal Ocean's waist pack. The otter who'd almost become mincemeat in the jaws of hungry alligators.

Tripp twisted his body to sling two handbags over his shoulder. "I have to finish my meeting with the osprey," he said. "So go on, Cam, practice your dance for later." He tapped the bells he'd hung around her neck. "Are you my little cutie pie?"

Camilla's laughter gurgled merrily. "Yes, Tripp, trippydy Tripp."

With immense joy, Tripp watched her toddle off to a corner, the tip of her tail pointing upward and waving like a flag.

He remembered cradling her tiny body, so fluffy, so cuddly, so soft. And when she had peeked out into the world for the first time and saw Tripp, her face lit up the swamp like a million fireflies, and his heart exploded, stunned at the intensity of his love. Since their parents abandoned them, he acted as both mother and father to her, a role he took seriously.

He returned to the river's edge, where a statuesque osprey raked her claws on the sandy ground, annoyed at having to wait for him.

"So," Tripp said, "you're going to do me this favor, right? I saved your kids during that hurricane, so you owe me."

"Yeah, I got it," the osprey said. "What do you have against the human boy anyway?"

"He tried to kill me! Then he sent me off on the slough where an alligator family invited me for dinner—*as the main course.*"

All he'd wanted was the boy's purse, Tripp thought. He hadn't deserved a death sentence, to be ripped apart by ravenous gators.

The osprey yawned. "I'll gather the troops. After this, I don't owe you anything."

She soared to the sky, soon joined by several other ospreys.

A few yards away, three of Tripp's friends practiced synchronized swimming. They rose from the water, raised their arms, and dipped back down. Their legs shot out and scissored. They submerged again, then two of the three leaped into the air like dolphins.

Tripp mentally went through his flawless plan to get back at uggy boy. His mouth moved as he rehearsed the words he'd say to him. His eyes twinkled at delightful thoughts of revenge. His body swayed to the tune playing in his head. He stopped abruptly and waved to somebody heading toward him.

It was Peeka and Boo.

Peeka sported a gray-haired wig he'd stolen from an elderly woman asleep in a beige Town Car. Boo had colorful cornrows with extensions that slapped his body and face as he jogged. One purple bead at the tip of a braid swung straight for one of his nostrils and got stuck there. He snorted it out, no problem.

"I knew I could count on my friends," Tripp said.

"What are—"

"—friends for, babe?" Boo sounded like a cool dude.

Tripp frowned. The more he knew them, the more he thought them strange. Yet they could write English, having found the alligators' schoolroom a few years before. Through a tiny peephole sculpted by a rat, they'd spent every day learning to read and write, abilities that came in handy for creating maps and signs to trick humans.

"I want uggy boy hurt. The spider I set up didn't work. Getting him into the panther's home didn't work. And the gator trap didn't work. So this plan *has* to work."

"At least that python can—"

"—have the gal." Boo twirled his beads.

"Oh, and what a monster! But he didn't get them at the tree island because that gator saved them. We may have to do something about him too. He can't be protecting them like that."

"You think the pythons are the—"

"—reason there aren't many of us left?"

"How would I know?" Yes, it was odd that pythons, Nile monitors, and other exotic animals roamed the Everglades. That wasn't any of his business. All he cared about was his family. Everyone else and everything else was not his problem.

One of the three river otters swam up to Peeka, silently sneaking up behind him. He snatched the wig from his head and volleyed it back and forth with the other two. One tossed the wig sky-high, landing it on the head of a flying brown pelican.

Peeka pouted. "Hey, you're salty—"

"—like sea otters."

"Don't waste your energy!" Tripp yelled at his friends. "We have a job to do soon."

Tripp opened the two purses. "Here's your share from the two bags I found near the airboat accident. I had to fight for them, stealing them from an opossum and her eight kids." He handed over an assortment of items: raw nut bars, charcoal toothpaste, a stapler, wart remover. He kept most of the loot for himself and his sister, rationalizing that he deserved more.

"What happened—"

"—to the people?"

"Are they—"

"—dead?"

"Don't know and don't care. The airboat was empty."

Peeka squeezed the charcoal toothpaste and rubbed his teeth. Boo stapled two cornrows together.

Tripp shook his head. "You guys have to stop letting your girlfriends mess with your hair. You're starting to look like them." From one of the purses, he unfolded a yellow rain hat and put it on. He then retrieved a red lipstick, lathering it unevenly over his mouth as he gazed into a hand mirror.

"I think this gives me some color, don't you?" he said.

Peeka smiled, teeth black from the charcoal.

Boo dabbed wart remover on his nose and said, "Looks hot."

Tripp danced again. "This plan is going to be stupendous! Uggy boy is going to be so upset."

"We get—"

"—a pond apple pie too."

"We should all watch and party!" Tripp yelled.

"Yes, that'll be—"

"—fun."

"But we'll have to do something," Tripp cautioned, "about that strange gator and the other humans coming down the river. And I have just the plan."

TWENTY-SEVEN

A Salty

It was late morning or early afternoon by the time we got to the marl prairie. That area was different. Patches of grassy plants covered parts of the pockmarked limestone. The jagged ground jabbed my naked feet, making it difficult for me to keep up with the others. A short distance away, dark clouds loomed.

Boom! Lightning struck. I felt that rumble through my whole body. A Florida bear fell out of a tree and rushed away. He had a circular bald spot on his butt, just the size of Peeka's toupee. No way. It couldn't be.

We raced to a small cluster of shrubs and trees, moving along the edge of one to avoid being the tallest target for the lightning.

The faster I walked, the faster the limestone sliced my feet. In pain from bug bites, tired muscles, grazes, bruises, and now my feet, I wasn't sure I could make it to the river.

I needed to think positive. Once we *got* to the river, I planned to lie on the bank and soak my poor feet. Our parents would find us there for sure. We'd be back home, guzzling gallons of clean water, eating regular meals, sleeping in a soft bed. Who knew the basics were so important?

Ellen glanced over her shoulder and noticed I was lagging. "Hold on, guys," she said.

While she waited for me to catch up, she half smiled at my dirty, tattered shirt. Her gaze drifted to my feet.

"Ocean! You're bleeding!"

"It's fine. I can handle it," I said even though my feet throbbed miserably.

Nano reached over the carrier. "Ocean!"

He flicked his tongue as though he wanted to lick my cuts. Yeah, no thanks. I knew where dogs licked. I didn't care if their saliva had healing stuff.

"Are you okay?" Gumbo asked.

"Yep. The limestone cut my feet, that's all. It's fine."

Once I reached Ellen, she crouched down and peeled off her shoes and socks.

"Here, please wear these." Without looking at me, she handed me her pink socks.

"No thanks," I said but took them from her.

"Ocean River, listen to me and put them on, please." She continued tying her shoes, avoiding eye contact.

"All right." I placed my hand over her head as if casting a spell, not like a wizard but vampire style. "You never saw Ocean wearing pink girly socks. Blah, blah, blah."

"Oh, you sound just like our bat friend, Count Batz," Bix said. "He's a hypotist."

"Hypnotherapist. For past-life regression therapy," Gumbo said.

That was interesting—and bizarro.

I sat on the ground and took my time easing the socks onto my painful feet. I hoped the soft cotton would help.

Having Ellen deal with my cuts reminded me of when we were six or seven years old.

Ellen and I had been at a playground with Mrs. Hansen. Ellen went down the slide first, and I followed. When I reached the bottom, I fell forward and smacked my forehead on the hard surface. Skin split. Blood splattered.

Mrs. Hansen rushed over to me.

At the top of the slide, Ellen stared in shock at my bloody shirt and head.

"Why weren't you watching him, Ellen? He's always watching over you." Mrs. Hansen pressed my wound with a tissue. "You have to be all eyes. Be more responsible. Focus, Nena. Focus."

After that, Ellen would get nervous whenever I did risky things, which was often. I still had the scar on the left side of my forehead, covered by my bangs. I never thought much about the incident, but maybe that was why she'd become so serious and why *focus* was one of her overused words.

With the socks on, I stood up and said, "All done. Let's get going."

Ellen spun around and took off, head down.

"How's your arm?" I asked.

"It's fine. We have to keep moving."

I hurried to get next to her, wanting to check her expression and her wound, but she sped ahead.

Great. Something was up.

We finally reached the river, which seemed like hours later and after blood had leaked through the socks. Being so tired, my legs shook and my arms felt like twenty-pound dumbbells.

The open space had red mangrove trees. To our left and right stood more of the same, but in denser groupings, while behind me, white mangroves covered those areas.

Ellen and the others watched the smoke near the marl prairie blow into the sky. Since park rangers monitored brush fires, I hoped that would bring a chopper.

"When you go home, Ellen," Bix said, "you and Ocean will be best friends, right?"

I waited for her to say something positive. Nothing. Not a word. Things had been going well between us until she saw my feet. At least she cared enough to give me her socks.

Bix and Gumbo exchanged confused looks.

Whatever. I dragged myself toward the river, too tired to think or care.

"We could set up a sign for planes and helicopters," Gumbo said to me.

"I'll get some sticks," I said tonelessly.

"Are you not feeling centered?"

"Just tired," I mumbled. Tired of trying to prove I was responsible and mature. Tired of trying to earn Ellen's forgiveness. Tired from hiking all day without much food or water.

I started to gather sticks. After that, I could soak my feet and rest.

Wanting to be alone, I moved to the river's edge. I smelled the otter again, but I didn't care anymore.

Red and black mangrove trees lined both sides of the river with only a few narrow open areas.

The water was brackish, a mix of salt and fresh water. I didn't know if we could drink it because the water meandered down the river, and gross-looking clumps of junk stagnated around its edges. I knew that algae could be toxic and bacteria and parasites could also kill us, so I didn't want to take the chance and drink it. Gumbo might know if it was safe.

Maybe we could all pray and send out positive vibes just as the late Dr. Emoto had done with people over a polluted lake. Apparently, the water changed. But I didn't have the energy, and I didn't feel positive right now.

I glanced up the river. If no one showed up here, we could build a raft and go north. Going downstream would take us to the ocean, and that'd be worse. Too bad mangroves hung off the river's edge, leaving no walkway.

I wasn't sure about the terrain next to the river either. It could be lined with gators or impassable brush. Well, at least we were safer here than in the middle of the Everglades.

"Hope you have time to catch a python," Bix said. "I want you to be the next king!"

"I'm not sure I'd make a good king."

"Of course you would," Ellen said. "You're smart, strong, and protective. That's a king."

They said hello to someone. It was a young female river otter, wearing bells like those worn by one of my small rescue dogs.

"I need to practice my song and dance. Can you tell me if it's any good?"

"We'd be honored," Gumbo said.

Bix signaled to me. "Come watch, Ocean."

"Fine." I might as well take a quick break. As I started to walk up, Bix went back to watching the young otter. I laid the sticks on the ground.

"*Stuffity face, la, la, la.*" The little otter belted out a cha-cha song.

Out of nowhere, four river otters jumped me—one being the stinky otter who'd stolen my waist pack. He had lipstick all over his mouth like babies playing with makeup. Before I could yell, he stuffed my mouth with something yellow that resembled Mom's rain hat.

With his paw tightly over my lips, he whispered in my ear, "Did you know a family of gators tried to eat me because of you? You're getting what you deserve, uggy boy."

The singing otter pumped up her volume and banged rocks together, creating a racket. "*Grabidy legs, la, la, la. Dropidy ground, la, la, la.*"

I flailed my arms to get someone's attention, shifting right, then left. When an otter grabbed my ankles, I keeled over.

"*Knockidy head, la, la, la. Dragidy body, la, la, la.*"

One of my attackers bashed my head with a rock, and I became dizzy. Everything turned purplish gray, and my body felt even more tired. They lugged me into the water, rolled me onto something like a log, and covered me with weeds. I couldn't fight anymore. I was going to pass out at any moment.

"You're a salty, not a sweetie," the otter whispered in my ear.

"*Pushidy log, la, la, la. Swimidy fast, la, la, la.*"

I blacked out for the second time.

TWENTY-EIGHT

Ocean Gone

"*And fly, fly away, la, la, la,*" sang the young river otter, finishing on a long high note.

While we clapped, she slipped away before we could thank her or advise her. She had a great sense of rhythm and a lot of enthusiasm, though I wasn't sure about the choice of lyrics.

"Ocean, wasn't that fun?" Bix asked.

We all twisted around.

Nano whimpered. "Ocean gone."

Ellen ran toward the river. "Ocean?"

A pile of sticks, including his walking stick, lay near the water. Where was he?

"Ocean, this isn't funny!" Ellen yelled.

"Don't panic," I said, hyperventilating.

"I'm not panick—" She turned around to me and soothingly patted my shoulders. "It's okay, Gumbo. He couldn't have gone far. Maybe he's gathering more sticks somewhere."

After I stopped wheezing and choking, I said, "I'll check underwater." I didn't know what else to do. I sensed something terrible had happened to him.

"Do you think he's in there?" Ellen cast a worried glance at the river.

"No, just making sure all is well." I didn't want to frighten her, but yes, I was concerned that a gator or python had dragged him into the water. With the young otter hitting rocks together and singing loudly, we could easily have missed something.

"Okay." Ellen ran along the river's edge. "Ocean! Ocean! Ocean!"

Ellen's call sounded nervous. She had every right to be. We hadn't been watching the otter long enough for Ocean to have vanished completely. The river's edge revealed no blood—a good sign—but oddly, no footprints either. The sandy surface might have been brushed with a palmetto leaf, just like the leaf that floated nearby. Something didn't add up.

I dipped under the cool water tinged by tannin from the mangrove leaves, my eyes accustomed to its tealike color. Lying motionless to avoid stirring up muck, I scanned in every direction. No boy, no gator, no python. Several species of fish drifted by, studying my every move.

A gar floated just under the surface. He opened his mouth to say something to me. Right before he could speak, an osprey swooped in, lifting him straight out of the water.

I resumed my search under weeds, rocks, mangrove roots, plants, and muck.

Nothing for twenty feet in every direction, I swam back to Ellen. What would I say to her? It was my fault. I should have been watching over him.

There is no one to blame.

Someone was to blame. Shoulders heavy, I trudged out of the river, and Ellen rushed over.

I shook my head. "Sorry, Ellen. I should have been aware of my surroundings and protected Ocean."

"It's not your fault, it's mine. He's been taking care of me this whole time, saving my life, while I did nothing for him. Maybe he left me." She held back tears.

Nano and Bix hugged her ankles.

"Ocean would never leave you," I said. Why would she even consider that? Ocean cared about her.

She turned her back to me, perhaps to wipe her eyes.

"I'll check farther down the river. I'm sure we'll find him soon." If he wasn't in the river, he had to be somewhere in the mangroves.

By the time I submerged again, Asha started to sing "Everything Will Be All Right" at an acceptable decibel. She sang it to me whenever I experienced a difficult challenge.

Do not worry. Do not cry.
Never let your spirits die.
Keep your chin up to the skies,
Trusting everything will be all right.
You will always be where you are meant to be.

Learn from every situation.
Stay on path to its fruition.
Keep the faith, don't fall apart.
Let your love comfort your heart.
Everything will be all right.
Everything will be all right in the end.

As I cruised down the river close to the surface, I checked above and below for signs of Ocean. Then I reached a narrow canal where mangrove trees formed a tunnel. A tricolored heron admired his reflection in the water's mirror.

"Namaste. Did you see a young boy in the river?"

"Nope. Didn't see a thing." The heron didn't even look at me.

I swam to a red-bellied turtle, sunbathing on a fallen tree trunk. Shimmering engine oil floated around him.

"Namaste. Did you happen to see a young boy?"

"No, we're sorry," the turtle said.

A second head lifted after the other head moved out of its way. "We'll let you know if we do."

After thanking the two-headed turtle, I swam farther south, increasingly more anxious because no one had seen Ocean. I stopped to speak to two alligators resting on the bank. A third gator joined them.

"Namaste. Did you see a boy go down this river?"

"No, although we saw river otters pushing a mound of weeds that way," said one alligator, pointing south.

"Yeah, that was strange," said another.

"Thank you."

Pressing even farther south, I noticed several river otters playing with Peeka and Boo. Among them, the otter I'd saved carried what appeared to be two human purses. He tucked them behind him and narrowed his eyes as I got closer. Oddly, he had red paint all over his face.

"Namaste, Peeka and Boo," I said. "Have you seen Ocean?"

"No. Maybe—"

"—he flew away."

They erupted into laughter.

"Thank you," I said and headed back to Ellen.

I sensed some connection between the otters, the raccoons, and Ocean's disappearance. Peeka and Boo had insisted on a specific route. Was it a coincidence each location harbored dangers? Asha had always said there were no coincidences. Perhaps my anxiety over losing Ocean skewed my perception.

As I glided through the water, I prayed Ellen and Asha had already found him. Then I stopped moving when another thought disturbed me. What if Ellen disappeared too? I swam as fast as I could.

TWENTY-NINE
Can't Handle It

I slowly opened my eyes. A cloud of wings flapped around me. My body floated in the air, feeling light and cool.

"It's about time you woke up!"

Who said that? My vision cleared. Carried in a net by at least twenty or more ospreys, I stared in shock. How did I get here? I looked down. What! I could fall!

"Well?" A green anole on my chest hopped closer to my face.

Startled, I cried out, slipping on the fishing net when I jerked. The anole straddled my face and hung on to my lips as the net shifted beneath me.

The ospreys panicked and dipped sideways, heading straight for a stand of hardwoods. I locked my fingers on the net. They flew higher, saving my Sasquatch from smacking into trees. The anole slipped into my shirt.

We jetted between heavily wooded areas, scattering brown pelicans from their roost. Spotting a pelican wearing a gray wig, the ospreys and I gawked. It looked just like the wig from the car on US 41. It fit better on the pelican.

I turned my gaze back just as we were heading straight toward a double-crested cormorant perched on a tree. His eyes nearly popped out.

Flapping their wings as fast as they could, the ospreys finally rose but slammed into a flock of white pelicans. They tussled with the white pelicans before separating.

When the ospreys on my left lost their grip, I slid left. When the ospreys on my right dipped down, I rolled to the right. We leveled off just as the Florida Bay came into view.

"What's happening?" The anole peeked out from under my shirt. "What are they gonna do with us?"

"In case we fall into the water," I told him, "you should get inside my shirt pocket. It's waterproof and EMF-proof."

"Wait, you answered back and I understood you! You speak lizard. And what's an EMF?"

"Electromagnetic fields."

"Whatever." The anole zipped himself into my pocket.

Deliberately and with control, the ospreys descended to where the river flowed into the ocean. At the height of maybe twenty feet, they spread the net, hoping I'd slip out, and when I didn't, they rattled the net, but I clung on. I flopped around, lost my grip, almost fell, then caught the rough mesh again.

"No! Take me back!" I shouted, holding on tighter.

The anole came out from my pocket. "I'm getting

dizzy." He nearly fell out, so he crawled back in and zipped up again.

They kept swaying the net, and my fingers started to bleed.

One last swing loosened my raw fingers, and I fell into the seventy-degree ocean.

The chilly water shocked me. My feet hit bottom, stirring up sand and turtle grass. Small stingrays, hidden underneath the sand, scampered away.

A nurse shark resting on the bottom started moving toward me, probably drawn by my bloody feet and fingers.

I rose to the surface, oriented myself, and headed toward the shore.

Bottlenose dolphins swam nearby—and the shark swam closer too.

What would I do if the shark attacked? I had no energy left. My swim strokes became slower, weaker.

"I *can't* handle it." Salt water stung my eyes, but my tears washed it away. My legs cramped. My arms hung like anchors, pulling me down.

"What's going on?" the anole yelled from inside my pocket.

I took in a big gulp of air before I sank. Peaceful sunlight radiated from the surface down into the water. I closed my eyes, feeling almost comforted under the blanket of gentle waves.

The shark bumped my arm to test me.

If he bit me, I wouldn't be able to do anything. It didn't matter anyway. I'd be dead in a day or two, alone on the beach without clean water to drink. He'd save me from a slow, miserable death.

Floating and sinking, I felt a sudden swirl—dolphins. Two knocked the shark away from me while another dolphin scooped me up from beneath and pushed me to the surface, heading toward shore.

In the shallows, the dolphin flipped me over so I could swim a short distance and stand up.

I swam and sloshed onto the sandy beach. Exhausted. Emotionally worn out. I couldn't form words to thank them. I tried to lift my hand, only to have it rise a few inches. Still, I spoke to the dolphins in my mind. They bobbed their heads before swimming away.

For now, my only goal was to reach a tree and rest a few minutes in its shade. Then I'd figure out a plan to get back to Ellen.

THIRTY

Kindest Person

At the wide mangrove river, I splashed out of the water, searching for Ellen. She was safe in the corner with Asha.

They hastened toward me.

Before Ellen could ask, I said, "Nothing south. It's like he disappeared into a parallel universe."

She covered her face for a moment, then spread her hands, frantically pacing right and left. She opened her mouth but no words came out. Then she blurted out incoherently in a tearful and trembling voice that reminded me of myself.

"Pushed him. Afraid to hurt him. Like Dad. My fault. He takes care. Brave. Bloody feet. I'm a bad friend. Bad person."

Nano, an expert at monosyllables, translated for Bix. They hugged her ankles, and she knelt to pet them.

"You're a good person," I said. "Ocean too."

Ellen shook her head. "It's all my fault. Ocean might be dead because I didn't watch over him like a good friend. You know, my dad died in an accident because of me. And

Ocean almost cracked his head open when I was with him years ago."

A Miami blue butterfly fluttered behind Ellen before resting on a red mangrove. I'd only seen one before when I was a child.

"It's not your fault, princess," Nano said, sounding different than usual.

"It's no one's fault," Asha said in the gentlest voice she could. She wrapped her soft wings around Ellen.

"Ocean is the kindest person I know." Ellen wiped her wet eyes. "He'd visit Mrs. Abrams every day after her husband died because he didn't want her to feel lonely and sad. Then when his neighborhood friend, Lamar, became paralyzed after diving into a pool, Ocean spent time every week, making him laugh and helping him with whatever he needed. He even made him the drummer in his band. Ocean would give me his shirt if he thought it would help me."

"That poop-dyed, mud-stained, ripped shirt?" Bix smiled wide, eyes sparkling. "I want it."

Nano shook his head.

"Don't give up hope. He might be north on the river or somewhere around here," I said. If we still couldn't find him, I didn't know what to try next.

Wait. I inhaled sharply. Something had changed. I scanned the area. "Never mind. I should stay here with you in case there's danger."

"Please, Gumbo, could you check up north?" Ellen stepped closer. "Then you'll have covered the whole river. We'll be fine here. We still have to check more mangroves to the left and right."

"Okay." Even though I didn't want to leave, she was right about searching north. At least we'd know for certain. I glanced around again before I made my way back to the river.

"Believe all is well and trust," Asha said to Ellen as I slid into the water. I needed that reminder myself.

I swam and prayed again to find Ocean safe. After a few minutes, I felt focused and calm, my mind cleared of its incessant chatter. As I weaved through the water, I explored every section of the river, making sure I missed nothing.

My senses told me he wasn't this far north, though I hammered on, just in case. Not a moment later, a group of kayakers came south. Our prayers were answered! But then they turned around and headed back north. *No!*

I charged toward them, screaming, "Wait! Please don't go!" Of course they couldn't understand me, and my excitement only made things worse.

The kayakers frantically paddled up the river. The lead human yelled into a gadget. I couldn't translate all the words, except *stop, tours,* and *gator's nest.* He must have told them to stop all tours because of an angry gator protecting her nest on the river.

Though pursuing the kayakers was pointless, I swam north anyway and searched. As I headed south again, I saw several signs hanging from trees lining the river. Stay Out. Gator's Nest. Do not pass or you'll die.

I didn't see any other gators and *do not pass or you'll die* didn't sound right. Except for royal families, most alligators couldn't write English, and even then, the penmanship was barely legible.

The handwriting and paint matched the hiking trail sign at the bayhead tree island, and those didn't match the typical Park Service notices. Did Peeka and Boo make these? Sometimes I smelled raccoons near our school, so I wouldn't be surprised that some could write.

I searched the area nearby for anyone who might have done this. It was empty.

Was this the end for my new friends? If they didn't get help today, I'd have to carry Ellen and Nano on my back up this river. Since kayakers had come down this way, there should be humans north. Although Ellen would likely be stubborn and refuse to leave without Ocean, I'd have to convince her that it was our only hope, our only chance of finding help.

THIRTY-ONE

Lighten Up

On the beach, I slumped under a tree and tugged off Ellen's socks to let them dry. The salt water had almost healed my cuts but not the pounding pain. My head and sunburned skin hurt too. Within a couple of minutes, the heat and my aching body got to me. I felt myself dozing off.

I woke up to find at least fifty laughing gulls watching me. A few gulls started giggling, then it was ten of them, then twenty, and a moment later they all were laughing hysterically.

The anole on my shoulder and I laughed too, even though I was obviously the butt of some joke. Hermit and mole crabs scampered around me, cracking up. A passing bee couldn't contain himself, tittering and tee-heeing as he buzzed over me.

When I stood up, they all stopped laughing and flew away. I searched for signs of people, boats, and campers. Nothing.

As I plodded through piles of dead seaweed, a swarm of tiny fiddler crabs blocked my way. They moved left, then right, all the while staring at my huge, swollen feet. One macho crab showing off his big claw attacked my big toe.

"Ouch!" I hopped in a circle, only to step on sand spurs—those prickly, pea-sized burs with pointy thorns that made them difficult to remove without stabbing one's fingers. I grabbed a broad leaf from a nearby vine and sat down to carefully pluck the burs from my feet. Once they were off, I went back to get Ellen's socks and sat to put them on.

Once done, I hugged my knees. What should I do now?

The green anole jumped down from my shirt and faced me from the ground. "Fine mess you got us in. Hey, like your hairdo?" He pointed at my head and laughed. "I thought it might be funny, and yes, it is."

"Are you the same anole from before, when we were on the airboat?" I used my fingers to comb through my hair and caught a bunch of flowers and plants that had been woven into it. The back of my head was painful to touch.

"Yes. My name is Iggy."

"Ocean River."

He smirked. "What kind of name is that?"

I ignored his question.

"Aren't you wondering how I got to the river?" he asked, going underneath my shirt.

I didn't really care. Stuck alone on the beach, far away from Ellen, I was in the worst possible situation.

Iggy opened my waist pack. "First, after you guys took off in that airboat, an osprey grabbed some branches with me on them. Second, he chatted with other ospreys—*yap, yap, yappity, yap*—and before I knew it, I found myself by the mangrove river. Then third, I tickled the osprey between his toes, and he dropped me. After that, your angry otter friends put you on that driftwood where I was napping in the corner, and you know the rest."

Yeah, the stinky otter. How was I supposed to know an alligator would capture him for a meal?

Iggy squeezed into the opening of my pack, then came right out. "Thanks for saving me some food."

"I didn't."

"Yeah, no kidding," he scoffed. Next, he checked the sand around a sea grape shrub near a couple of drift logs.

"Well, she wanted me far away from her, so here I am!"

"She? Oh, that pretty girl. Your girlfriend?"

"She's not my girlfriend."

His face brightened. "Maybe she wants a pet lizard."

"I tried to show her that I've changed by taking the lead like a mature, responsible person."

"Did that work?"

"I made things worse." I moaned and rubbed my forehead. "I should have worked together with Ellen—as a team like we used to—instead of trying to prove myself."

"Stop whining. Lighten up! Things will get better."

Iggy's eyes widened when a young dock roach scurried around an iridescent multicolored shell. "Problem solved," he said as he chased after the roach.

"Now she probably hates me because we got separated. It's all my fault."

The roach escaped into a hole in a drift log. "Problem not solved!" Iggy leaped after the roach.

"Mom said to forgive others for hurting us, so I guess I'll forgive her for not liking me and let her go for good."

"Problem solved!" Iggy yelled from inside the log.

"But I want her to like me!"

"Problem not solved!" Iggy shouted desperately.

"You know what?" I sighed. "She doesn't have to like me. My parents always said some people will hate me because they have hate in their hearts and not because I was hateworthy."

"Problem solved!"

"I need to live in the present moment and forgive the past, including my mistakes and hers."

Iggy climbed out of the hollow log, cleaning his mouth and smiling contentedly. "What are you yapping about?"

Jumping to my feet, I sprinted to where the river emptied into the sea, and Iggy followed.

Black mangroves extended beyond the land, which left me with only one choice: I'd have to swim up the middle of the river.

I wondered if Ellen was worried about me. "Did you know how much I cared?" I murmured.

From the edge of the bank, Iggy said, "Well, I didn't know you cared, but that makes sense. I'm so wonderful and handsome and smart. I don't want to bore you, but I could go on and on."

"We need to go back up the river."

"Excuse me? First of all, you're the only human here. Second of all, there's no way you can swim all the way back up."

"I can get help."

"Why don't you just wait here? A boat should pass by someday."

"I'm not the type to wait around." Dad taught me that hopes, wishes, and goals were useless if we didn't take action and work hard toward reaching them.

A chopper's rhythmic blades thrummed the air overhead.

"Hey! Over here!" I rushed back out toward the ocean's beach, away from the few trees and shrubs at the river's mouth so they could spot me.

A flock of cattle egrets soared to the right of the chopper, and both egrets and chopper headed northeast, the opposite direction of the river.

Think, Ocean. Think.

A few yards away, brown pelicans were diving for fish.

"Hello!" I called out. "I need your help."

Two pelicans flew over to me. I knelt on one knee to be on their level to discuss my plan.

Once they left, I saw the dolphins who'd saved me. "Dolphins! Hello!"

They swam toward the beach, diving in and out of the waves as they approached.

"Hello!" the dolphins said in high-pitched voices.

"Thank you for saving my life before. I need your help again. Can you take me up the river? My friend's life is at stake."

No questions asked, they said yes in their cute baby voices.

"Please meet me over there."

They flipped their bodies sideways and swam to where I pointed.

On my way to the water, I found a square piece of driftwood—perfect for my plan.

"Easy, boy." Iggy followed me. "What are you up to with those dolphins?"

I picked him up and placed him atop my head. "Hold on to my hair or go inside my pocket."

"I can't swim. But I want to see what you're doing."

Like a boogie board, I straddled the driftwood and swam to the middle of the river.

"Maybe I should go into your pocket," Iggy said.

Two dolphins flanked me, and the third dashed to my feet. Without a word of instruction, they understood my plan. They were definitely among the smartest animals.

"I know that helping me up the river will be hard. I promise to help dolphins even more after I get home."

The dolphin behind me pushed the soles of my feet, thrusting forcefully with his torso. The other two swam alongside, ready to take the pusher's place when he got tired.

"This is suicide." Iggy circled my head while pulling my hair.

"I'm going home!"

"To the cemetery!" Iggy screamed.

We *whooshed* up the river past a manatee with boat propeller cuts on his back. What was he doing out here all alone?

A group of ibises perched on black mangroves watched us curiously. One skimmed next to me before lunging for my waist pack. It could be the same ibis from the road before this whole misadventure began.

"Bad bird! Bad bird!" Iggy yanked my hair harder.

The ibis started to go after him, so he jumped safely into my shirt pocket and zipped it.

We veered right, close to a stand of black mangroves. *Whack!* Their branches slapped the ibis into the water, then he flashed out when a jaw-snapping crocodile chased him.

Crocs.

I glanced around. Sure enough, one croc slid into the water, heading right for us. Another followed, then another. Not good.

Next thing I knew, the dolphin spun me around and forced me left. A second later he shoved me right. The crocodiles were trying to bite me! The dolphin steered me straight, zigzag, and sideways.

Then the dolphin behind me slipped off my feet, and I got dunked. Once I resurfaced, two crocodiles faced me, ready to snap. A bold dolphin knocked them both away.

I grabbed my driftwood and kept swimming north.

"Iggy, you still alive?"

Iggy shouted from inside my pocket, "Barely. Good thing the EMF was protecting me."

A crocodile popped up in front of me again. A dolphin immediately bumped the side of his head. Unable to see what was happening underwater, I could only imagine the three dolphins' struggle against the relentless crocodiles.

Once again, a dolphin pushed my feet, and we were traveling upriver. While I couldn't say what happened to the crocodiles, clearly the dolphins outsmarted them. Crocodiles have tiny brains; dolphins, big ones. Yeah, even so, crocs have survived longer than most animals.

Later, when we'd reach the brackish water, alligators might want to attack too.

Scratch that. I concentrated on positive thoughts. Maybe Ellen *and* my parents were waiting for me. Wouldn't that be fantastic?

THIRTY-TWO

Be Still

Sun rays highlighted a white mangrove. Gentle waves stirred purposefully in that direction. Curiously, someone had lit candles near the tree, creating an inviting space.

Be still.

I needed to meditate for a few minutes before I went back to Ellen, so I didn't care who had left the candles. I couldn't face Ellen with the bad news. Not yet anyway.

Once I reached the tree, I crouched in a lotus pose, calming my breathing into a steady drumbeat. One, two, three, four. A few minutes of mindful meditation would do me good. Then I'd be ready to tackle the next step.

As I tried to quiet my mind, the ego stepped in. I was a loser, not a winner. If I couldn't protect just one child, how could I protect the Everglades as their next king? Not only had I failed Father, but I might also have killed two innocent humans. I'd be banished forever. Perhaps I'd live the rest of my life in disgrace.

Remember who you are.

I am a divine spirit. Nothing can truly hurt me because I am eternal. I inhaled a deep breath and began to breathe steadily, watching my abdomen rise and fall. I closed my eyes and observed the negative thoughts drift across my mind without judgment, without emotion. After just ten minutes, I felt calmer and stronger.

How could I please Father and save my human friends?

You have everything you need.

Physically I was capable of the highest level of performance. During my short stint in the military, it was clear that no one came close to my strength, not even Cyp. Perhaps that explained his increased bullying. He knew that if we ever had to fight for the throne, I'd win the battle—if I wanted the crown. Which, of course, I didn't.

Before we lost Mother, I'd thought of myself as brave. But the guilt and pain at not being able to help her had cut me deep. According to my psychiatrist, it was during that incident and the swarming of spiders and snakes when the guilt and fear of critters took hold. How could I shake them off and be free? I'd tried and failed. Every time I thought of Mother, I cried. Every time I saw spiders and snakes, I froze.

Yet I *had* gotten better at facing my fears after being with Ocean and Ellen. Caring for them gave me courage. Their bravery also inspired me.

You were always brave.

Even though I was only a few feet long when I lost Mother, I had wanted to fight the men, so I wasn't a coward. Yet I'd let fearful thoughts and uncontrolled emotions limit my life.

From what I'd learned, our brains "rewired" after we thought and acted in a certain way, making it easier and faster to respond in the same way the next time. The brain didn't judge whether our thoughts and actions were beneficial to us or not. It was merely programmed to help us get there quicker. That was why I became paralyzed, why I plunged deeper and more readily into panic and anxiety as years passed. Those were my go-to responses.

Saving Ocean and Ellen from the alligators and the python had given me confidence, so my brain must have rewired itself again. I needed to learn more about this, but for now, I should face my fears. Keep thinking good thoughts. Keep taking action toward my goals. Keep focusing on the present and stop going to the past to hurt myself. I also had to stop worrying about the future.

There is nothing you cannot do.

You are unfolding as you should.

It's time for you to step into your destiny.

"Om . . ."

THIRTY-THREE

Monster Show

The dolphins swam much slower in the brackish water. The lack of buoyancy exhausted them. "This is it," I said. "I can take it from here."

The mangroves around us formed a tunnel by reaching for each other from both sides of the river. Cool.

"Thank you, dolphins. I owe you guys." I loved them so much.

"You're welcome!" they said, and the weary dolphins dove back into the river, on their way south.

With barely any strength, I swam the sidestroke until I reached the familiar wide area. I was back. *Phew.*

Once I lumbered out at the river's edge, I took off the wet socks. My legs felt like forty-pound bags of birdseed.

"You okay, Iggy?"

"Yeah." He clambered out of my pocket. "Where's the pretty girl?"

Yeah, where had everyone gone? I must have been away for a few hours, so maybe they moved to another location or had been rescued.

In the red mangrove forest to my left, I spotted Asha, stepping carefully among their arching roots.

Before I could call her, I found Ellen coming out from behind some thicket near white mangroves, and I sighed.

Then something else caught my eye, and I froze.

The jumbo python slinked out from a shrub, heading right for Ellen.

"What a freak of nature!" Iggy jumped into my pocket.

"Greetings. Wish I had a bottle of Dom Pérignon. You'd pair nicely with it."

Ellen shrieked, whirled around, and sprinted toward Asha.

I tried to yell, but I could only croak, and my legs felt pinned to the ground.

"Uh . . . Uh . . ."

"What's wrong with you?" Iggy crawled out again to get a better look at me.

Bix and Nano appeared from behind a tree, gaping at the massive python undulating past them.

"Biggie Mouth and still a stranger danger," Bix said.

Asha's foot got wedged between mangrove roots, and her left wing gyrated like a broken metronome at four hundred BPM.

Ellen shot a glance over her shoulder and tripped to the ground. She turned around, massaged her ankle, and pointed her walking stick at the python.

"Uh . . . Uh . . ."

"A delectable, sweet girl." The python must have stared at her long, dark hair, because he added, "That might cause a hairball."

Once the python got closer to her, my body felt zapped with a bolt of energy and my feet loosened.

I sprinted. "Ellen!"

"What are you doing?" Iggy yelled. "You're supposed to go in the opposite direction."

"Ocean!" Ellen cried.

I grabbed my walking stick, lying exactly where I'd dropped it.

"Stay away from her, you—Burm!" I growled.

Bix and Nano jumped up and down, clapping and trying to whistle.

"I just supersized my dinner!" the python said. "I prefer to feed on you first, so I'm delighted you showed up."

"You okay?" I asked Ellen.

"My ankle's sore, but I'm fine. I thought I'd lost you." She reached for my hand as I helped her up.

"Yeah, almost," I said and glanced at her while we slowly backed away from the python.

She gave me that once-familiar expression. Now I knew what it meant: admiration. That boosted my energy even more. I could handle Biggie Mouth.

The python slithered in step, staying within striking range.

"Where were you?" Ellen asked, staring nervously at the python.

"Swimming with dolphins. Well, to get back from the ocean. I'll tell you about it later. Where's Gumbo?"

"He went up the river to search for you."

Asha finally disengaged from the roots and hauled herself toward us.

Iggy popped out, smiling at Ellen. "Hi, beautiful."

"Uh, hi."

Eyes rolling, the jumbo python waggled his head. "I'm starving here!"

Iggy zipped back into my pocket.

In a flash, the python dragged me to him with his tail and twirled his upper body around mine, all before anyone could sneeze. Now I knew how it felt to be crushed by beefy football players.

Iggy unzipped himself and came out panting. He climbed to my shoulder and bobbed with this dewlap swinging at the python—this time it was a threat.

Ellen whacked the python on his head.

He loosened his grip. "That's a surprise." He slapped her on the back.

She took the full impact and fell.

"Ellen." I barely got her name out.

"It was nice knowing you," Iggy said to me.

Asha stabbed the python with her stick. He hit her, and she soared thirty feet away.

"Asha!" Ellen jumped up, appearing okay except for dirt and red marks on her face.

Nano and Bix bit the python, who recoiled in pain before smacking them. "You'll be dessert later."

Ellen screamed. "Nano! Bix! Are you all right?"

The little guys answered by jumping up and racing

toward the python. Nano had gotten braver since yesterday morning. And Bix? I never imagined him a fighter, but his bite drew blood.

Ellen sprang toward the python, and he slammed his tail against her stomach before she could hit him. She bent over, trying to catch her breath.

"There's no way you all can fight this python," Iggy said.

Asha ran back like a ballerina running on the tips of her ballet shoes while being chased by a horde of elephants. She knocked the python and me on the head. The python flung her farther away than before.

"Asha, you hurt?" Ellen yelled.

Asha shook her head and ran toward the python again.

"You won't get a chance to kill him, because we'll stop you no matter what it takes." Ellen charged toward the python, and he tripped her with his tail. This time she fell on her butt with a thud. Then with one sweeping motion, he threw Asha, Bix, and Nano into the mangroves.

"Unlike other pythons, I can eat him and still fight all of you," the python said. "I'm that special."

The lack of oxygen was making me lightheaded. My worst fear—dying inside a python—was about to come true. The thought of being slowly dissolved inside the python's body made me want to puke. Or maybe it was him squeezing those awful pond apples in my stomach. I'd bet pond apples didn't go well with my blood type. I'd have to ask Mom.

"Just sit back and enjoy the show," the python said. "None of you are a match against me."

"But I am," Gumbo growled in a deep, powerful voice. For a moment his voice even scared me.

I swam to shore, heart racing at the thought of my friends in danger. Despite my fear, I rose to my full height, steadying myself before racing toward them.

"Gumbo!" Ellen yelled.

"Gators are much stronger than you," Ocean said breathlessly to the python. "And Gumbo is even stronger than others. He can beat you for sure."

Ocean's face turned bluish when the snake squeezed tighter.

"I'm the strongest animal in the Everglades!" the python yelled.

"You won't prove that by . . . killing kids and small animals." Ocean wheezed heavily. "Only weaklings and cowards . . . do that."

"Let him go!" A tiny green anole raised a fist. "Fight the gator, you monster."

When I reached the python, he sneered and released Ocean.

"I just saved your life," the anole said to Ocean.

Right away Ocean's face regained its color as he staggered toward Ellen and the others.

"One last thing," Ocean said. "Breath mints. You need bags of it."

The python gave a silent snarl.

"Or munch on a bag of potpourri," Ocean added.

I stepped in front of Ocean and Ellen to face the python.

"Try a breath spray. You'll need a tankful."

Destiny certainly had a way of forcing me to face my fears. I could simultaneously save my friends and capture a python more than sixteen feet long. The question was how to do it without killing him.

"You want a piece of me?" The python shimmied his upper body and head. With no arms or shoulders, he looked strange doing it. "Pathetic gator, I'm the top predator now. I'm the king of the Everglades!"

"What did you say?" I growled. That riled me. I couldn't remember a time when I'd been angry.

"He called you a pathetic gator," Bix said.

"King of the meanies!" Nano pointed a threatening finger at the python.

I drew myself up even taller. "Alligators are and *will always be* kings of all the swamps, including the Everglades." These pythons acted as though they owned the place, just as Father had said. Prodigious eaters, the pythons had consumed almost all the mammals and wading birds in the Everglades, and now they wanted to rule? Never!

The staccato beat of a chopper drummed from a distance. It grew steadily louder, possibly heading this way.

"We're going home!" Ocean sounded excited, as though he knew for certain.

"Ocean and Ellen," I said, "please step aside and let me take care of the python."

They moved away while they clapped and whistled.

"You got it, Gumbo!" Ocean said.

"Woo-hoo!" Ellen yelled, and then oddly, she repeatedly punched the sky with one fist.

I bowed to the python, inviting him to make the first move.

The python sprang toward my legs. I jutted my body forward and back faster than he did, and he hit a tree, missing me by an inch. I ended up in a backbend, then in a mountain pose, and faced him again.

Next, the python streaked toward my head. I flipped myself away into a handstand, and the python slammed into a red mangrove where he panted. Getting him tired would work. That way, I personally wouldn't have to kill him, yet I could defeat him and capture him once his energy depleted.

"Are you hurt?" Ellen asked me.

My legs and chest hurt. "I'll be okay. How's your arm?"

"It's infec—"

"Gumbo! You hit the jackpot!" Bix clapped and hollered.

We whirled around and gawked at a shocking scene.

A hundred—maybe two hundred or more—young pythons, one to four feet long, slithered toward us, wicked-looking and hungry.

Iggy said, "A jackpot? More like a monster show."

"A few of my children to join in the feast. Their mothers are rock pythons, mean and strong, and I date several of them," the python said proudly. Then he struck Gumbo's legs.

Gumbo fell but quickly jumped over the python's body. I shifted my gaze between the jumbo python and his children. Using yoga poses, Gumbo made the python miss him again and again. He moved fluidly while the python looked like an erratic yo-yo. Smart Gumbo. He hadn't touched one nasty scale on the python, but he was tiring him out. We could do the same to the python's children.

To our far right, an alligator showed up, then dashed back out.

The young pythons surrounded us, so I placed Nano and Bix into Ellen's carrier.

I grabbed Iggy and slipped him into my left pants pocket. "Iggy, you should be safe in there. If something happens, it'll be easier for you to jump down from there rather than from my shirt pocket."

Asha, Ellen, and I dropped into warrior I and II yoga poses and brandished our walking sticks for the fight.

"Let's work together and flip them into a pile," I said. "Eventually they'll be wanting their nappy time."

Ellen and Asha nodded.

"I need a nappy time too," Bix said.

The jumbo python continued attacking Gumbo. He bit Gumbo and wrapped himself around him. Gumbo rolled on the ground, trying to loosen the snake's hold. I couldn't worry about him right now. He had to deal with that one while we took care of the children.

Using what I'd learned from Asha last night at the tent, I cleared my mental jabber, took deep calming breaths, and swept the young pythons into a pile at the center of an open space.

"Kiyap!" I yelled.

"Kiyap!" Ellen gave me a single nod.

We kicked forward, dancing in our own unique way, slapping several pythons at once. With concentration and a quiet mind, my supernatural abilities came through, and time seemed to move slower. As I twirled a few snakes with my stick, I could see the next three groups shooting toward me. Within a second or two, I got them all before they got me.

Energy rose from the base of my torso, speeding my legs and arms as if a fast-forward button controlled them.

Unreal. To anyone watching, we probably looked like superheroes.

In case Gumbo needed me, I occasionally checked to make sure the python wasn't overpowering him. They were still rolling, and when they stopped, Gumbo chomped down hard on the python's body so he could untangle himself.

I couldn't imagine Gumbo ever hurting anyone. I guess if he had to, he would do what was necessary to save lives.

The young pythons kept attacking. We shuffled faster, tossing them into the mound, now a few feet high.

Two pythons wrapped themselves around my already hurting calves.

Ellen grabbed them using both hands and chucked them toward the others.

After several minutes, half the pythons slept or lay tired, and the others moved much slower than before. Because of that, we got the rest of them into the pile faster.

That gave me time to talk to Ellen. "The chopper is getting closer. It should be here soon."

"We're going to be all right," Ellen said.

"I'm sorry for everything. I mess things up—rarely, of course." I smiled.

She laughed. "More like often."

We stared into each other's eyes, meeting as best friends again.

"Ouch!" A baby python nibbled my injured toe. I pushed him gently to the heap and returned to the pesky young snakes still coming at us, though much slower.

"You know I never meant to hurt you." I cleared two pythons away. "Am I forgiven?"

"I already forgave you." She teared up again. "I'm sorry I hurt you too. I just needed some time to grieve. You know, I'm still in shock and not over my dad's—" She choked on the words and stopped for a second to sweep four pythons away. "And I had too much to do at home. We couldn't pay the bills. Mom was crying every night. I had to focus and get more serious."

"If that's even possible!"

She flipped more pythons as she laughed with tears in her eyes. "I haven't laughed since, you know, until I came here with you. Isn't that terrible?"

"True." Nano nodded.

"That's terrible!" Bix said.

"I can make you laugh." Iggy winked from my pants pocket. "I'm Iggy. Want to take me home?" His red dewlap swung out, making him look colorful. Show-off.

"We're having a special moment here!" I said.

We sped up, pushing more pythons into the pile.

"Can you forgive me?" Ellen asked.

"I'll think about it." I winked, then I got serious. "The past is gone. The future isn't here."

"All we have is now," Ellen said. "I get you, Ocean River. You're the most wonderful guy I have ever met."

I smiled like a goofy, happy horse. "Thanks!" I ramped up my dance.

"Kiyap!" Ellen joined in and tried to best me.

"*Thanks?* That's all you have to say?" Iggy shook his little head.

Honestly, I had no clue how to respond. She thought I was the most wonderful guy she had ever met! That compliment went way beyond my goals for this trip.

"Look over there, Ellen." I stopped and pointed. Gumbo's mean brothers and a commanding alligator— tall, bulked up, and walking on his hind legs, probably the king—appeared from the nearby mangroves. A small crowd of alligators followed behind them.

"Go help your brother!" the big gator said. Yep. The king.

"I pulled a muscle in my arm," the muscular brother said, clearly lying.

"I have a stomachache." The shorter one rubbed his belly. That could be the truth. He seemed a bit different from Gumbo and the other brother.

The king shook his head.

Gumbo hadn't seen them yet. With his back to them, he rose, then lifted the python and hurled him against a mangrove tree.

From my peripheral vision, I saw a bunch of pythons flying into the air. I turned back to the young pythons. Vines twirled around them and cinched them together. The skinny panther who'd chased Ellen popped up and waved to us in a friendly way.

"Want to play tag again?" he asked Ellen.

"No thanks! I'm good."

"I've been trying to stop them too," the panther said, pointing at the pythons.

"Thank you," I said. I felt bad for him, traveling long distances to search for food. I was glad the jumbo python didn't get him.

The panther used a handful of twisted vines like a lasso, swinging it, roping a few pythons together, then flinging them into the stack, now over four feet high.

Our fight was done. He'd catch the rest of them, so I glanced over at Gumbo. Wow.

THIRTY-FOUR

Hello

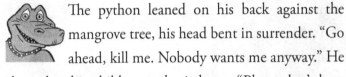 The python leaned on his back against the mangrove tree, his head bent in surrender. "Go ahead, kill me. Nobody wants me anyway." He glanced at his children and cried out, "Please don't hurt them." His eyes glistened.

Unharmed, the mountain of young pythons lay sleeping. I stiffened when I saw the panther from the mossy hammock forest. But Ocean and Ellen seemed unafraid, and the panther acted friendly and helpful. When a baby python woke up, the panther growled in his face, and the baby immediately passed out from fright.

"Gumbo!"

I spun around. "Father!"

Not far away, Father, my brothers, and dozens of other alligators stood gawking. I had no idea where they'd come from or how long they'd been there.

Father raced toward me. When he reached me, we hugged, a bit awkwardly. A flood of emotions radiated from my chest, and my eyes watered.

He released me and held on to my shoulders. "Our junior king!"

I nodded. "I'm sorry I couldn't kill the python."

"Perhaps you can help me come up with another plan."

My brothers joined us.

"I'm proud of you, Gumbo," Father said.

Cyp whipped his head to look at Father, then glared at me.

Father patted my shoulders. "You won both awards as I knew you would."

"Can you show me some of those moves?" Will asked. He contorted his body, only to trip and fall on Cyp.

After I helped them both up, Cyp elbowed Will.

The helicopter hovered above us, swirling sand all around. I tilted my head back and waved like an inflatable tube man during a hurricane. It looked like our parents! Even though they couldn't hear us, Ellen and I yelled, "Hello!"

The chopper circled to find a spot clear enough for landing, and soon the engine shut off somewhere close. Ellen and I couldn't stop our smiles and tears. It was all over. We were going home for sure.

The brown pelican with the jagged scar on his beak joined us.

"Thank you!" I waved.

He bobbed his head.

"Is he the same pelican from the airboat?" Ellen asked.

"Yep. I asked two pelicans to find him and tell him that the boy who helped him with the plastic bag is in danger and to ask him to perform the mosquito dance for any chopper in the air and guide it to the widest section in the mangrove river."

The brown pelican slurped up a young python. It wiggled helplessly in his expandable jowls.

"You saved us, Ocean," Ellen said. "Thank you."

"We saved each other. We're a team."

Iggy shook his little head. "Sappy stuff." He slipped deeper into my pants pocket.

All the young pythons lay drained. We stared at our accomplishment, something we could never have done without Asha, Gumbo, and Yaha's gift.

The panther continued adding more snakes to the pile, then he wrapped them up with an artistic arrangement of vines. Were the deer sculptures his creations? Probably.

The pelican swung his right wing to say goodbye.

Ellen and I returned the wave before he lifted into the sky and headed south.

Iggy climbed out of my pocket and settled on my shoulder. He held my photo in his mouth, the one with Ellen and me sticking our tongues out and crossing our eyes.

Ellen handed Bix to Asha, then took the photo from Iggy, her smile mixed with tears. "I missed you so much." She reached out and hugged me.

"I didn't miss you at all." I chuckled.

"Hmm, not boyfriend and girlfriend," Iggy said.

We pulled apart, blushing.

"We're just friends, and we turned twelve a few months ago," I said.

"Sure." Iggy didn't believe me.

"You're a tiny little thing, aren't you?" Ellen said to Iggy.

"I'm a large, formidable lizard." Iggy bobbed his upper torso, red dewlap out, then stood up and stomped around like a scary velociraptor. Yeah, good try.

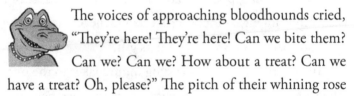 The voices of approaching bloodhounds cried, "They're here! They're here! Can we bite them? Can we? Can we? How about a treat? Can we have a treat? Oh, please?" The pitch of their whining rose higher as they neared.

A moment later two forest rangers arrived on foot with the bloodhounds on the far side of the clearing, trying their best to control the excited animals.

At the same time, two biologists I'd seen a few times around the Everglades drove up in a utility truck, and all the alligators, except for my family, disappeared.

The female biologist studied some sort of gadget before glancing up and waving to Ocean and Ellen.

"Hi! Are you kids all right?" she said.

"Yeah, we're fine! Our parents are in a chopper nearby," Ocean said. "All these animals are our friends." He then pointed to the pythons and said in a gentle voice, "Please take the Burms." He bent his head to stare at the empty ground.

Ellen touched Ocean's shoulder, matching his lowered head. And Nano touched Ellen's arm.

I mourned for the python and his children too. It wasn't their fault they were here, and now they'd be killed.

One ranger grabbed a snake hook from his backpack while the other tied the dogs to a tree. They tiptoed toward the mutant python. Without resistance, the python let a ranger grab his neck. The other ranger lifted the python's massive body.

The female biologist carried several large burlap bags toward the young snakes. The other biologist, who was much younger, hurried toward the mutant python.

"Louis?" he said. "It's Hugh."

The python, Louis, stared quizzically for a moment, then his eyes widened before narrowing to threatening slits. He lunged at the man named Hugh, but the rangers held him back.

"I'm sorry, Louis," Hugh said. From what I could gather, he knew Louis and truly cared for him. Words such as *college*, *changed to biology*, and *looking for you*, were all I could figure out.

As if trying to discern whether Hugh was telling the truth, Louis studied his face. Hugh pulled a battered heart-shaped toy from his shirt pocket.

Louis stared at it, tears streaming down his face. Hugh wiped them. With a pleading look, Louis glanced at his children.

"Don't worry," Hugh said. He used other words: *safe* and *sanctuary*.

My heart warmed, happy they'd found each other. Though I still wondered if the python's kids would grow to his size. Also, where were his women? Prolific breeders, they could be pregnant somewhere, guarding their eggs.

With effort, the rangers lifted Louis's body while Hugh draped the head on his shoulders.

As they carried Louis toward the truck, the truck's engine roared. From behind the wheel, the panther waved goodbye and drove off. The men power-walked after the panther, Louis still in their grip.

"Hey, stop! That's FP 222," Hugh said.

"He can drive?" Ellen asked, shocked.

"Anything is possible." Ocean smiled.

Everything did turn out all right in the end, as Asha had always reminded me. *All is well.*

THIRTY-FIVE

Dreams

With bandages on their heads and arms, our parents sprinted toward us, keeping a wary eye on the alligators and waving to the men. Lots of hugs and kisses ensued, of course, and my parents kept looking at Iggy, who watched the exchange from my shoulder.

"I don't know what I'd do if I lost you." Mom kissed my forehead for the tenth time but not my pimply cheeks.

"My lacrimal glands are working overtime!" Dad said, wiping his tears.

"I love you both so much!" I cried. "You won't ever hear me complain about doing homework or cleaning my room or drinking wheatgrass juice!"

I cried harder, thinking about Mr. Hansen. How could I deal with my parents being gone forever?

Iggy whispered, "Mushy stuff again."

"*Te amo*. My Nena." Mrs. Hansen held Ellen's face.

"You're all I have, Mom," Ellen said. "You're the best mom, taking care of me, working two jobs—" She burst into that same hiccup-cry I'd done. "I love you so much!"

"I wouldn't have survived without your doing all the chores and being there for me. Oh! Hold your doggies!" Mrs. Hansen pinched her nose. "Stop and smell your clothes. You need a bath!"

Mom's eye twitched. Those clichés I knew. It was "hold your horses" and "stop and smell the roses."

Our parents handed us water canisters, and the water tasted *soooo* good. I'd never thought of clean water as delicious, but it truly was. I also rinsed off Iggy.

"Kids." Mom pulled something from her bag that smelled incredible. "I made a couple of those veggie burgers and sweet potato fries you like so much." I'd gotten a whiff of it the moment I'd seen her twenty feet away, but I thought it was my imagination!

Ellen and I exchanged glances before wolfing down the food. My visualization of this very meal and the chopper finding us here at the river had come true like magic.

While we ate, we learned that when the airboat later crashed into a tree island, our parents got knocked out, but the biologists—the same ones here—saved them. They didn't sustain any major injuries, and until our parents woke up this morning in the hospital, the police didn't know about Ellen and me. We also learned that Mr. Dale had been arrested. He didn't have the required training and had no right to take us out.

"That was genius," Dad said, "sending the dancing pelican from the airboat. Your mom knew right away you'd sent him. But how did you find him?"

I burped and just for fun made it last as long as I could. Bix giggled in the distance.

"Excuse me," I said. "We'll tell you all about it later, but first a doctor needs to check Ellen's wound."

"It's starting to really hurt." Ellen rolled up her sleeve— definitely infected, burgundy and black in several spots. I couldn't believe she'd hidden that from me.

"Ah!" Mrs. Hansen said. "You got cut like a scissor."

Cut like a knife? Mom's eye twitched again as she and Dad leaned over Ellen to get a better look at her arm.

After everyone had finished discussing all kinds of possible treatments, I said, "Hey, want to see dark purple and blue mushrooms?" I lifted one foot.

Mom and Dad yelled, "Oh no!" Both my parents crouched down for a closer look at my injured feet.

"Want some cranberry pie?" I lifted my shirt so they could see the zits, welts, and rashes.

They yelled again, but this time they took a step back. I had those things on every inch of my body—and they itched like crazy.

"The chopper will take us to the hospital," Dad said.

Mom pulled me to her and touched her head to mine. "You're both incredible survivors."

"You passed with glowing colors," Mrs. Hansen said.

"It's *you passed with flying colors.*" Mom finally corrected her. Maybe she'd stop twitching.

"That too!" Mrs. Hansen said. "But yours is a cliché."

I smiled. Mrs. Hansen knew what she was doing. She was smart and funny that way. Oh, and she made the best *pastel de tres leches* and flan in the world.

"Dreams come true if you truly believe in them and are persistent at achieving them, no matter how many failures it takes to get there," Asha had instructed me many times. Ocean and Ellen had visualized their parents on a chopper saving them, and here they were. I didn't understand Ocean's dad talking about the pelican, but I sensed Ocean had something to do with bringing his parents to the river.

I had visualized Father being proud of me, and here he was doing just that. Although I didn't seek out the python, destiny made sure I took action toward capturing him so that Father would be proud of me, which was what I wanted. Unfortunately, he selected me as the junior king. I'd never wished for it, but Asha told me that sometimes, we have to go with the flow, at least to accept it for now. Things may change later.

A junior king's position first required grueling instruction and physical training for more than a year. After that, I wasn't sure what else it entailed, except to assist Father and to learn how to be an exemplary king. If I failed, the next eldest son, Cyp, would take the throne.

I glanced at my brothers. Will bestowed a smile and a wave at the humans while Cyp glowered.

When I turned back to Ocean and Ellen, I noticed movement on the other side of the river. Peeka, Boo, and the river otters were snooping around a mangrove. They seemed to be up to something. I kept my eye on them, not wanting any more trouble.

"Good job, Gumbo," Father said. "For making friends with humans. We need their help to save the Everglades."

Cyp clenched his jaws.

"Yaha gave them the gift to communicate with us, but they might lose it when they go back home."

"You can read and understand English, so I don't see a problem," he said. "But you could also learn human sign language with your new friends. That might be the best way to communicate."

Sign language was a great option.

"The king of Big Cypress will want to meet you," Father said. "An alliance between our two families through marriage is the next step after your coronation in a year or so."

"That's *if* he passes all the tests," Cyp said.

Father gave him a quick side-glance. "He will."

Cyp glared at me again.

My mind was reeling. A loveless, arranged marriage in a year or two? That practice was so outdated. Our royal families should be able to marry anyone. Why force me to do this? I wanted to find love the natural way.

Be present. Be here.

Yes, that was in the future. The only time is *now*.

Handing the water canisters back to Mom, I said, "We have to say goodbye to our friends."

Dad stared at Gumbo and his family, his eyebrows meeting his hairline. "You're friends with those animals? I've never seen gators like that. Are they ancient aliens?"

"We'll explain later. You're not going to believe everything we've done and seen."

Our parents nodded uneasily.

"We'll be okay," Ellen said.

I took her hand, and we strolled toward Gumbo. As we got closer, Gumbo's father and brothers stepped aside to give us space.

"Thank you, Gumbo, for saving our lives," I said. "We'll never forget you."

"Just another day in the enchanted Everglades." Gumbo bowed with hands in prayer.

"You leaving?" Bix whimpered, looking sad for the first time since I'd met him.

"We'll miss you." I rubbed Bix's shell. "We'll come back and visit."

"Great! We had fun, didn't we?" Bix said with a smile.

That was more like it.

"Fun!" Nano yelled.

Ellen touched Gumbo's arm. "You'll make a great king, Gumbo. The world needs smart yet kind and compassionate leaders like you."

Gumbo bowed again. "You both taught me a lot. Thanks for being good friends."

I felt an odd tingling in my head that reached all the way down to my injured toes.

Asha stared above us.

"Is Yaha going to take away his gift?" I asked.

"*Neeak, neeak, neeak, enaaaaye, enaaaaye*," Asha shouted.

No!

Iggy covered his ears and said something, but I couldn't understand him either.

"For talking out loud," Mrs. Hansen said. Mom's eye must have twitched again because Mrs. Hansen added, "You need to see a doctor about that eye tic."

It was true. Yaha had taken back his gift. What a bummer. Ellen and I exchanged disappointed glances.

We squished together for a group hug.

When I felt the tingling sensation again, I quickly checked Asha. She stared above us, then at Ellen, before her gaze shifted to the mangroves.

"I didn't get the chance to let you know how to find us," Gumbo said.

"We can understand you again!" Ellen squealed.

"My mapdar would have found you," I said.

Silence.

Then we all burst out laughing.

Ellen and I touched our heads together and made cross-eyes, sticking our tongues out just like in the silly photo.

All of us except Asha and Iggy twirled defective mapdars on our heads. Iggy shook his pointy head as though we were mental.

"Asha," I said, "why is Yaha letting us keep the gift?"

"I told him he might need your help someday," Asha said.

Definitely we'd come back to help—and bring earplugs.

Ellen and I were animal talkers, maybe even shape-shifters. I didn't know what it would bring to our lives, but it had to be positive, at least for animals in need. My pets at home—four dogs, a cat, a mini pig, a fox—would get better attention too. Even though I'd try to keep our talents a secret, it'd be impossible because they would understand us as soon as we spoke.

At least we'd be free to talk to animals in the Everglades without a hassle. We'd visit again very soon and spend time with our new friends and make new animal friends. I'd be able to properly thank the dolphins. I'd bring help to the panther. I'd track down a certain river otter.

Asha stared at the mangroves, then at the sky and waved.

We all waved too, assuming Yaha was floating across the trees in search of Eleanor. I wondered how we could help him. If Asha couldn't convince him that his love was dead and in heaven, how could we? Anyway, we'd find out in the future.

"The time is always *now*," Asha had said.

After what I'd gone through, I didn't want to waste time worrying about the future or living in the past and ruining my life right here, right now.

And right now, my wishes had come true. The problems Ellen and I had gone through made our connection stronger. With our new shared talents and abilities, our friendship could never be broken again, right? All the tears and lessons had been worth it, and I felt more mature and a better person. Though I was ready to go home after the hospital and sleep for days.

Gazing at my friend for life, at my new animal friends, at my family, at the strangers who'd come to rescue us, I smiled. The *now* was where I wanted to be.

I am here in the present.

The End

"Thank you for reading our adventure story.
Please join us on social media."

Ocean, Ellen, Gumbo, Bix, Asha, Nano, and Iggy

 @EnchantedEverglades

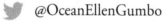 @OceanEllenGumbo

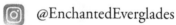 @EnchantedEverglades

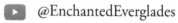 @EnchantedEverglades

#EnchantedEverglades
#BePresentBeHere
#IamHereInThePresent

EnchantedEverglades.com

SPECIAL THANKS

Family and Friends:

Thank you for your time, energy, and love.

Eleanor S., Katherine A., Rosalie K., Helen N., Trevor S.
Katherine K., Roxana V., Wendy M., Camilla D., Hector M.,
Edward K., Alex K., Stephen S., Laura L., Jonathan C.,
Cindy L., Alex & Monika B., Kristina M., Carolyn S., Ray S.,
Tracey D., Richard K., Miles H., Lynne H-C., Alvina Q.,
Steve & Stephanie F., Rosemary E., James M., Brent B.,
Michael C., Stacey M., George S., Gerry & Olga S., Karen J.,
G. Brian B., Angie G., Sunny & Anu G., Alisha G., Steve S.,
Ian B., Mindy D., Gisela C., Elizabeth D., Louis V., Jill K.,
Nicole A., Bill G., Gina R., Lily C., John W., and others.

⚜

Influencers:

Thank you for inspiring me to create stories.

God, Jesus, Ellen DeGeneres, Oprah Winfrey, Dr. Wayne Dyer,
Deepak Chopra, Helen Schucman, Martin Luther King, Jr.,
Rumi, Gandhi, Eckhart Tolle, Louise L. Hay, C. S. Lewis,
Stephen Simon, Michael Goorjian, Mikki Willis, Paulo Coelho,
James Redfield, Kahlil Gibran, Dan Millman, Richard Bach,
"Two Listeners," David Hoffmeister, Gary Renard, Joel Osteen
Swami Sivananda, Dr. Kenneth Wapnick, St. Francis of Assisi,
Marianne Williamson, Tony Robbins, Andy Andrews,
Brian Tracy, Zig Ziglar, Og Mandino, Napoleon Hill,
The Wachowskis, Christopher Nolan, Robert Zemeckis,
James Cameron, Steven Spielberg, George Lucas, Pixar, Disney,
DreamWorks, J. K. Rowling, and other filmmakers, artists,
writers, comedians, and spiritual teachers of the world.

Editors, Reviewers, and Beta Readers:

Thank you for being a guiding light.

Karl Iglesias, Beth Hill, Mary Kole,
The Editorial Department, Victory Editing,
Eileen Robinson, Lynette M. Smith,
Phil Williams, Grace Kastens, D. Patrick Miller,
Isaac Marion, Joanne Fowler, Geri Morgan, Sandy Brock
BlueInk Review, Booklist, The Children's Book Review,
Foreword Clarion Reviews, Midwest Book Review, and
Kirkus Review

❦

Artists and Musicians:

Thank you for sharing your marvelous talents.

Tim Shinn, Anton Jaspard, Joe Badon,
Frankie B. Washington, Giles Crawford, Kevin Sacco,
Paul Hernandez, Ziv Music, Andy Ellis Valdini,
Ron Ochs, Eve Cuyen, Nathan Nasby, Gideon Nasby,
Ariel Petrie, Ezemdi Chikwendu,
and others from Airgigs.com.

❦

Angels of the Everglades:

Thank you for your conservation work.

Marjory Stoneman Douglas, George Bird Grinnell,
Earnest Coe, Guy Bradley, Arthur Marshall, John A. Marshall,
Judge William Hoeveler, Everglades Foundation,
Everglades Coalition, Audubon Society, Everglades Trust,
NPS, FWC, biologists, scientists, environmentalists, activists,
and many more.

G. A. KOWATCH lived in South Korea, Vietnam, and the Philippines before going home to the US at the age of thirteen. She has degrees in both design and business. Her first short film, *The Right Friend,* garnered several niche festival awards and was distributed by Spiritual Cinema Circle. Gail is an avid fan of movies, especially sci-fi, comedy, fantasy, thrillers, animation, and romance. This is her first novel.

Author's photograph by John Fernandez